I0678793

University

M.M. Bylo

© 2024 by M.M. Bylo

All rights reserved. No part of this book may be
reproduced or used in any manner without written
permission of the copyright owner except for the use of
quotations in a book review. To request permission,
contact the copyright owner at
marissabylo@gmail.com

This is a work of fiction. Unless otherwise indicated,
all the names, characters, businesses, places, events, and
incidents in this book are either the product of the author's
imagination or used in a fictitious manner.

Printed in the United States of America
First edition June 2024

Cover design by Victoria Lynn
Line editing by Ashley Earley

ISBN: 979-8-9893483-1-2 (paperback)
ISBN: 979-8-9893483-2-9 (eBook)

www.mmbylo.com

For the one struggling in the dark. That isolated place where destructive thoughts and habits reign and produce shame. There is no shame in this struggle, you aren't alone, and there is hope.

In honor and memory of
Kayla
Brandi
Madison
Isaiah
Hamilton

The Syllabus

The Syllabus

Author's Note

Dear Reader,

Your reading experience is more important to me. This book talks about heavy topics, so I wanted to include a trigger and content warning. I believe it's important not to shy away from these topics. However, my intention is NOT to blindside you.

This novel doesn't show the triggering events happening in detail but rather the reaction/aftermath. They are a real part of this book. There will be some of you who have experienced these horrific things, and you shouldn't have to relive them when reading. See below for warnings.

<3 Marissa

Trigger Warning: sexual assault (not in detail, some PTSD episodes), suicide (not shown), portrayal of mental illness (depression, anxiety, and some PTSD), and references to disordered eating.

Content Warning: fade to black sexual scenes (no foreplay or anything explicit/detailed), college partying, hookups, substance abuse, drug and alcohol usage.

Prologue

The only reason I'm going to college is because everyone else is doing it. It's a good kind of peer pressure, right? It's not like we are all jumping off a bridge together into an abyss. Even though it kind of feels that way right now.

Think about it: hundreds of young adults whose brains aren't fully developed stuck in close quarters with no serious supervision then expect them to know what they want to do for the rest of their lives. This can't be a good idea.

Complaining isn't how I should start this new season of my life, is it? The decision to attend college is mine alone. To be fair, that degree declaring "I'm enough" for a big girl job enticed me to commit a minimum of four years to something that's not a person. I'm drowning in thousands of dollars of debt already, but at least I'll have job security as a life preserver keeping me afloat. Besides, I don't have a choice, right?

Here goes nothing.

Chapter 1

Fall Semester
August 20th, 2014

Long, unruly weeds wave my maroon Honda Civic along the interstate like a guide to my temporary home—university. Wind rushes through the car's rolled down windows, filling it with that thick humid Midwest air; the intent is to distract my budding nerves. The drive would be easier if someone else was here, but it's only me for this road trip.

My phone chimes with back-to-back texts from Dad: "When does college start, Mellie?" and "Are you going to the community college?". I laugh at his attempt to remember the details of my life. He's trying though.

Mom's response to me leaving was tears as she helped pack my things into the back of the car along with a promise to call midway through the trip.

That was a few hours ago.

I check my phone at a rest stop, and instead she sends a text that reads: "Can't wait for you to intern. Remember it's paid." Of course she wouldn't call; being the founder and the current CEO of her marketing firm keeps her occupied.

Dad still doesn't pay attention, and Mom decided my future for me. How safe and predictable—my favorite things.

Staring at the blurring trees and seemingly endless road because that's all there is to look at around here, I try not to think about anything which is never successful. *Breathe, Melanie. You'll get to college soon and in one piece if those semis don't run you off the road first.* Only six hours of what-ifs and wondering if I'll regret leaving my hometown.

Tightening my hands on the steering wheel, I rehearse how I found myself here. The college's marketing team did a fantastic job boasting of its prestigious business school. After applying and receiving a substantial scholarship, the admissions counselor hyped it up like it was a full ride. Update: it's definitely not.

Hayley and Alex, my best friends from high school, stayed home to attend community college. They wanted to save money for the first two years before committing to university. I should have stayed home, too.

My boyfriend Brady could be sitting next to me, but he chose to be with his fraternity brothers this weekend. We've been dating for two years though we are completely opposites. Hayley and Alex often tease me about that fact.

With him being a college baseball player and obnoxiously charismatic, I can admit Brady is entirely out of my league. I don't need my friends reminding me that he and I fall into the "cool guy falls for nerdy girl" trope like some of my favorite novels; the books give me hope that someone like him could care for someone like me and stay.

Yet none of them are present on this momentous day. Brady won't lecture me about "living my best life". Hayley won't spill her daily latte, nor will I watch Alex effortlessly jump over hurdles during track meets.

My stomach folds into itself at the realization of what I am doing and where I am going—away from everything I've known for the last eighteen years.

Breathe in, breathe out. Repeat.

My heart rate slows to a normal rhythm, and I divert my thoughts from the fear of the unknown. This is my chance to start over. No one at the university knows me, so I can create a new reputation. No more "Melanie The Stagehand" or "Melanie The Yearbook And School Newspaper Writer and Editor Extraordinaire." *Okay, no one called me that. Ever.* I smile anyway, while snapshots of happy high school memories–yes, those exist–float through my mind. My fingers loosen their grip on the steering wheel for a mere moment.

But my mind betrays me today.

Nagging questions lurk, forcing me back to reality. What if I can't pass my classes? What if I can't make new friends? What if I'm alone? What if Brady breaks...I shake my head. Why do I have to ruin this new beginning with worst-case scenarios and nerves? *Come on, Melanie. Happy thoughts only. No tears today. I am an adult now. Better start acting like one.*

A green and white highway sign announcing my arrival to town interrupts the self-sabotage as I exit the interstate at the prompting of my cellphone's GPS. Instead of breaking down in tears, the rows of homes boasting antiquated architecture, cobbled streets and sidewalks, elaborate stone water fountains, and historical statues are enough to distract me. I drive along Main Street where petite boutiques and antique shops occupy much of the space while bars linger on every corner. The manicured landscaping ties everything together. This is my welcoming party.

After Main Street, campus unfolds in front of me as I drive under its historic stone gate, signaling the end of my road trip. I finally made it! Of course, the entire freshman class and I arrive together as I compete with other cars for a parking space. Across campus will have to do. I grab a handful of my belongings and trek to a freshman residential hall named Montgomery after a founding board member according to the student who gave me a campus tour last summer. Peers, parents, siblings, significant others, and students volunteering as movers push and swirl around me in a frenzied human wave. I dodge and apologize to everyone all the way to the dorm. The moment I walk through its front doors, a girl who cannot be much older approaches me with a clipboard and smiles down at me with all her teeth.

She wastes no time.

"Hello! Welcome to Montgomery Hall! I'm Taylor, one of your Residential Advisors or RA for short. What's your name?" Taylor asks in a shrill customer service voice as she grabs my hand and earnestly shakes it.

I wrap my arms around myself. "I'm Melanie Billow," I tell her.

"Nice to meet you!" Taylor scans her clipboard and waves me to a small locker inside the Resident Director's room directly across the hallway from the lobby. Her toothy smile remains as she grabs my room key amongst hundreds of others.

"Nikki will be at the mandatory floor meetings later this week. You'll love her," she explains as she leads me up the cramped stairwell. "Your roommate Sophia is already here. Lucky you're on the second floor. Same floor as me. It's going to be such a fun year!"

Taylor babbles about the dorm and rules–something about girl/guy floors and how this is a dry campus so no alcohol–but I'm taking in my surroundings. This floor has a lounge crowded with a microwave, couches, a round table with chairs, and two sets of large windows facing the parking lot and a hill behind the dorm. The hallway branches in both directions leading to the rooms. Hand-made decorations cram every inch of wall space. The second floor is winter-themed with construction paper polar bears and blue streamers dangling from the ceiling in contrast to the cinderblock walls and gray paneled ceiling. The RAs tried to make it look less like a prison.

I bump into Taylor. She stands in front of room 219, the space Sophia and I will share according to the hand-written name tags taped to the door. Dropping the room key into my hand, Taylor sprints to her next task. I take a deep breath and open the door to behold my stunning roommate and her family unpacking. Sophia looks over, raising her manicured eyebrows in greeting. I mutter a greeting and throw my bags on the empty bed and decide to retrieve my belongings rather than make small talk.

Trip after trip of weaving through wide-eyed freshmen and parents interrogating the RAs leaves me breathless. The headache and soreness forming in my throat slow my progress. An hour passes by, and I set my last box on the cold tile floor. I cross my arms and survey the space. *Now what? No one is around to tell me what to do and when to do it.* This independence is startling. For years, life was this predictable pattern: wake up, go to school, after-school activities, homework, sleep, and repeat. I found the monotonous routine comforting; I knew what to expect every day.

Breathe, Melanie. Do the next right thing.

I survey my half of the room brimming with boxes, bags, and storage containers; too much stuff for such a little area. Well, making my bed would be a logical step. A simple, predictable plan—that's what I need so I don't get overwhelmed by this unfamiliarity.

I wrestle a purple fitted sheet onto my bed; one corner flips up while Sophia unrolls a fluffy white rug on her side of the room. Neither of us have spoken to each other yet.

I swallow my nerves and say to her back, "Hi, Sophia. It's nice to meet you. Sorry I've been so busy with moving my stuff which is hard because it's just me—"

She doesn't turn around but interrupts my babbling. "Hello again." Her tone is uninviting.

How am I already messing this up?

"Sure is hot outside. We picked a perfect day to move in," I comment.

She makes a vague noise of agreement as she arranges gigantic pink pillows on her bed.

I will give her one more chance. "How far away are you from home?"

"I live twenty minutes from here."

Her voice sounds like a little songbird. Whatever. I hope she's dumb. It's unfair if you're gorgeous, have an angelic voice, and are intelligent.

Sophia presses the TV remote in her hand, but the television won't turn on. She keeps hitting the button and turns to her mom complaining about things not working already. I notice the TV isn't plugged in yet. *There it is! Maybe she's not so smart.* I turn back to unpacking and try not to laugh. I'll let her figure that out herself.

A restless sensation courses through my body as I unbox and organize my belongings. I make random observations to Sophia about the room, but she barely utters a word in response. Conversations between her family fill the silence. Whoever lives above us scoots their furniture along the floor, and people passing through the hallway chatter and laugh. There are no moments of stillness nor quiet.

Wow. I thought my first day at university would be more inspiring and story worthy.

Sophia and her entourage leave, mentioning an early dinner. My stomach growls, but I'm determined to finish setting up, so the room feels more like home. Rather than taking a much-needed break, I shove a curtain rod full of curtains into the window. The thick black-out curtains promptly fall on top of me.

Someone knocks before opening the bathroom door.

"Hey, neighbor!" someone–probably my suitemate– calls from the bathroom. The dorm's design includes four women sharing one Jack and Jill style bathroom with two sinks, one shower with a tub, and a toilet. Thankfully the toilet has its own enclosed room for some privacy; I don't think I'll get a lot of privacy during the next four years; too many people around here.

I break free from the pile of curtains to discover my suitemate standing in the doorway with her hands shoved in jacket pockets. She's a true ginger: red hair, pale skin, freckles, and all. Clasping my hands in front of me, I remind myself not to ruin this by making a redhead joke. Hopefully she doesn't see my utter failure with the curtains and the fitted sheet curled into itself on the unmade bed too. Apparently, the twin beds are extra-long here.

She waves with both hands. "Hi! I'm Erin."

"Melanie."

Erin's smile widens, creating dimples on her freckled cheeks. "Nice to meet ya. Where's Sophia?"

"Eating with her family."

"Good idea. I'm starving. My roommate checks in tomorrow before our orientation class."

"Do you know her?"

"Yeah, Jessica and I went to the same high school. Probably why they put us in the same room. We live about an hour and a half away."

"Awesome! Can't wait to meet her."

We fall silent. I catch a glimpse of myself in the mirror hanging on our door, and it only confirms the worst—my frizzy hair and eye makeup smudged from sweating. That body odor must be me too. *Oh gosh, what do I say next?* I want to make a good first impression since I'll be her neighbor for the year. Here I am overthinking simple conversation.

I smooth down my hair, wishing for hairspray. "Well, it's nice to meet you. We can catch up after I'm done unpacking."

Erin shrugs. "No worries! Oh, we should go to the events planned for us with Jessica and Sophia if you want."

I nod, grateful she didn't take my dismissal personally.

She continues, her tone upbeat. "Our bathroom door will probably be unlocked when we're here, so knock when you're bored. Don't mind visitors. I'm gonna get something for dinner. Good luck with your room!"

Erin leaves, and I turn to the curtains mocking me from the floor. Either independence isn't as marvelous as promised, or high schools could offer practical classes. My private high school, Our Living Hope, loves to spit out AP test scholars and honor students who can't file taxes or properly hang curtains just like every other high schooler.

Mom insisted I get a private education, and the only private school close enough was religious; most of the students acted like Christians during the week but did whatever they wanted when no one was looking. I avoided them–or more likely that they avoided me–and studied hard to pass the religious classes, which I did.

I struggle with the curtains until they miraculously stay up then tuck two corners of the too-small sheet under the bed and set a blanket and purple comforter on top. But I can only ignore my hunger for so long, so I cook some food in the second-floor lounge microwave. The floor teems with residents and parents forcing me back to my room with a steaming bowl of ramen and no one to talk to.

Well, my first day at college is basically over. Why hasn't anyone texted or called to check on me?

Loneliness and boredom soon find me. Erin had invited me to come over, but I don't feel like myself tonight, probably all the unfamiliarity and constant noise. Sophia hasn't returned either. *She's staying at home tonight, I bet. Will she do that all semester?*

I lay in bed, my thoughts inevitably wandering to what I would be doing at home: an evening swim at my mom's backyard pool with Hayley and Alex, cruising on winding backroads with Brady in his Jeep, or eating buttery popcorn with Dad while we watch some show about gold miners at his apartment.

But daydreams are far from reality.

I organize my room until the sun sets then shower to prepare for tomorrow's orientation. It starts early in the morning, so I go to bed sooner than usual. *Tomorrow is a new day. Things will get better once I meet more people and make friends.*

Sleep doesn't come easy. Thunder rattles the windows and flashes of lightning brighten the room. With each swallow my throat burns, and I shiver. I have no control over the AC or heat in the room.

Halfway through the night while staring at the ceiling, I give up on today and hope for a better day two.

Chapter 2

Sleep evades me. Hours of tossing and turning pass before an RA pounds on the door and yells, "Wake up, wake up! It's your first day."

Correction: four days stand between us freshmen and our first day of college classes. Until then we have a mandatory freshman orientation class and more events than I care to attend.

The pain in my throat and my whole body is not helping. I haven't moved from bed yet, my fatigued limbs complaining as I shift to grab my phone from the small dresser that doubles as a nightstand. Two messages pop up on the screen that I missed last night.

Hayley in a group message with Alex: "Let's swim tomorrow!"

Brady: "Back from camping. Call you this weekend."

I text back and explain to Hayley that I left for school then tell Brady I can't wait to talk with him about college.

Even though there's not much to report yet.

The bathroom is empty. *Erin must have left for*

orientation already. Will we be in the same class, I wonder as I finish getting ready, grab a protein bar, and head outside. Finding the class is easy—follow the massive group of chattering students to a massive building across campus.

I triple-check my schedule for the right room. My peers' voices fill the classroom while we wait for our instructors. I don't recognize anyone, so I sit in the front row between a cute guy with a distinct accent, and a muscular girl with wavy, black hair and thick-rimmed glasses. They talk with the people around them. Every inch of me is stiff, and the longer I sit in silence between them, the worse it gets.

Apparently, making new friends and small talk is not my forte. *Do you want to be alone this semester? Say something, dang it.* I glance to my right as the girl checks her phone. *Here's my chance.* I open my mouth to say something, but two older classmates burst through the doors.

Upperclassman #1 yells, "Hello and welcome to your freshman year of college! My name is—"

Upperclassman #2 echoes, "and I'm—".

I already forgot their names. My nerves and fatigue are ruining this for me. I can't keep anything straight.

In unison the instructors shout, "Are you ready for the best four years of your life?"

They receive lousy applause and sarcastic "whoo-hoos". I rub my temples, my body clammy with a headache and a dryness lingering in my throat.

That's not good.

Upperclassman #1 pumps his fist in the air. "Guess what, freshmen? It's time to learn more about your new home. You know what that means?"

Upperclassman #2 answers for us. "It's scavenger hunt time! Each table row is your team, so get up and introduce yourselves to each other."

A collective sigh emanates from my classmates. *At least I'm not the only one who doesn't want to be here,* I think as I take another sip of my water bottle. Our row stands and forms a circle. The guy with the accent steps forward, running his fingers through his dirty blond hair as he says, "Hello, I'm Philip. I'm from Zimbabwe and here to play for the school's rugby team."

The person next to him introduces themself and so forth. When it's the turn of the girl next to me, she crosses her arms. She says, "Daniela. I am from the country of Colombia before anyone asks about my accent." She sheepishly grins, giving us permission to laugh.

Then it's my turn. I smile with all my teeth in my best attempt to be personable. "Hi, everyone. I'm Melanie. I'm from—"

Upperclassman #1 whistles, and the groups become silent. He holds up a stack of papers.

"First team that turns in this sheet with the most correct answers gets three extra credit points on their first exam in freshman experience class."

A buzz begins around the room at the scavenger hunt's award.

"Extra credit means less studying. Losing is not an option." Philip instructs us as if this is some sort of sport's game. My team nods and makes noises of agreement.

Oh no. They want to take this seriously.

Upperclassman #1 hands the sheet to each group, and Upperclassman #2 flings the door open. To my shock, some groups run to their first destination; my group is not far behind them though. My head pounds as I try to stay in step with everyone, sweat beading on my forehead and neck.

"You don't look good," Daniela calls back to me. The whole group halts as I collapse onto a bench, trying to hide my labored breathing.

I clear my throat before saying, "Yeah, it's the heat and those stairs. Don't mind me." I hold my water bottle to my face, but it doesn't help the flushing.

Philip's distinct frown says everything he's thinking. "We need to keep going if we want to win. Melanie, ask an RA to take you back to your dorm. Daniela, stay here until she gets help. You can catch up with us."

Daniela shrugs as she joins me on the bench. What a way to meet someone.

"I don't have any of the RA's numbers. Or Nikki, my RD," I admit to her.

"We live in the same dorm. Nikki texted that she is

busy so someone named Taylor will pick you up," Daniela says after a long pause.

Wow, that was a quick reply, I think as I take another sip of my water. I look over to her. "Sorry for the fuss."

"Welcome to university, I guess." She laughs, and we sit in silence. At least she knows not to talk my ears off when I feel like I'm about to faint; perhaps she's as uncomfortable as I am talking to strangers.

Taylor pulls up to the curb in her car, and I thank Daniela who runs to find the group. Taylor croons at me like I'm a child as I open the car door and collapse into the front seat.

"You poor thing. And your second day of college too. I'll take you to the Student Health Center once you've recovered from the heat. Let's get you some stuff to help you from my room."

We drive past other groups hollering and pointing as they find the answers to the scavenger hunt's clues. At the dorm, I follow Taylor to her room on the opposite side of the second floor where she hands me a disposable icepack, small pack of aspirin, and a cold water bottle. We make the short walk back to my room.

Taylor says, "Sorry. That's all I have for you." She opens the door for me with her master key. "I'll drive you to the Student Health Center when you're ready. Don't want you walking when you're feeling so cruddy."

I take a quick sip of the new water bottle. "Thank

19

you," I croak out, the dryness in my throat not satiated by the cold water.

She gives me a pitiful smile as I close the door and crawl into bed, the icepack pressed to my forehead. Everything hurts. I'm not sure how long I lay there before my stomach lurches. I stumble out of bed to the toilet, my body shaking as I drop to the floor.

"You okay?" Erin asks as she peeks her head around the corner of the door.

Darn, I forgot to close it. I shake my head and hold it in my hands.

Erin clicks her tongue. "Yeah, you look terrible. Jessica is studying to be a nurse. Be right back."

Jessica appears next to me, her shiny blonde hair tickling my face as she leans down and touches my forehead with the back of her hand. She examines me up and down, assessing my current predicament.

She says, "Nice to meet you, Melanie. So, you have a fever for sure. I'm checking for strep. Please open your mouth."

She flashes her phone's flashlight down my throat and makes an affirming noise. "Yep, you definitely have some stuff in there. You should go to the doctor."

"Thanks," I whisper as they shut the door to their room, giving me space to throw up in peace. It never happens thankfully.

I crawl back into bed and swaddle myself in extra

blankets—a cocoon of sweat and regret. Time slips away. The sun sets. At some point, Erin and Jessica laugh in the bathroom. They must be getting ready for the block party tonight. Sophia appears and disappears several times without a word to me. At least her silence is wanted this time.

Taylor drives me to the Student Health Center on campus the next morning. They direct me to a nearby urgent care who gives me my diagnosis and prescribes antibiotics. A 102.5 degree fever and my first time getting strep throat stops me from attending any of the planned festivities and going out and meeting new people. I haven't even started classes yet, but college is already kicking my butt.

University: 1 point
Melanie: 0 points

Chapter 3

First Week Of Classes
August 25th, 2014

My phone alarm harasses me on Monday morning, bellowing and waking me from a deep, medicated sleep. It's only 7 a.m., so I tap the snooze button twice. 8 a.m. classes everyday seemed like a sensible choice at the time of class signups because that's what I did in high school.

I have regrets.

I habitually check my phone for messages—there are none—then the room for Sophia who is absent. *I guess she'll go home on the weekends.* I have a new roommate anyway: insomnia. Blame the now non-contagious strep throat or the fact I share a tiny room with a stranger in a town six hours away from my comfort zone. Regardless, I haven't slept well since moving here.

The week of move-in with its orientation and events passed by without my attendance. When I messaged my friends about my disappointment, Hayley said it would be best not to dwell on it and encouraged me to "start over" my first day of classes. I should take her advice, not wallow in pity but focus on the positives.

Dragging myself out of bed to the bathroom, I step on the scale and type my weight into the log I keep on my phone's notes app. I text Hayley and Alex: "Good luck today!" In response Alex sends me a picture of her and Hayley wearing matching outfits this morning. Apparently, they have the same schedule too. They were joined at the hip in high school, so I'm not surprised. Hoping he'll remember it's my first day, I message Brady "Good morning" too.

Erin yawns as she closes her door, joining me by the sink while I brush my teeth. I wave as a greeting, unsure if she is a morning person or a "don't talk to me before I had my coffee" kind.

She offers a grin in return. "Morning. Happy first day of classes."

I pull the toothbrush from my mouth and spit into the sink. "You too. Oh, thanks again for bringing me food while I was sick. And for telling Nikki at the second-floor meeting why I couldn't attend."

"Ah, no worries. Sucks you got sick and missed the events and meeting Nikki. She's awesome." Erin yawns.

"Didn't sleep well?"

"Nah. Jessica snores. Something about the 'anatomy of her mouth and nose.' Lucky for her she has afternoon classes on Mondays."

I laugh and quickly cover my mouth as Erin tries to stop another yawn which fails. We fall into a comfortable silence as she brushes out her tangled hair, and I meticulously apply makeup.

At least try to look presentable today, I tell myself as I dab concealer on that one pesky pimple by my nose. I'm stuck here for the next four years, so I better make a good impression with my peers and professors.

Erin breaks the quiet after brushing her teeth. "8 a.m. classes were a terrible idea," she admits as she flosses.

"Won't be making that mistake again. What's your major?"

"Psychology. You?"

"Business."

"Cheers to us, a future businesswoman and a guidance counselor. Ha! Have a good first day." She throws away the floss and adds, "I work at the front desk checking people into the dorm. Don't be a stranger and say hi sometime!" She opens the door to her room, and Jessica's snoring seems to echo through the bathroom.

This is the most we've talked since meeting. She seems pleasant enough, I think as I fight back another laugh.

My phone buzzes, but it's another picture of Hayley and Alex. I close my eyes and take a deep breath, pushing the negative feelings to the back of my mind as I face the first day of college in my jeans, free university T-shirt, and sandals. I sling my faux leather backpack onto my shoulders and grab a toaster pastry, my textbook in the other hand. *Time for Elementary Spanish II.*

Other students stumble through the dorm as mindless and tired as me. *I need to get my own coffee pot and some leggings. No one else is wearing jeans,* I observe.

The campus brims with activity: students walking, running, driving, and riding skateboards and scooters. Those with schedules pressed to their faces with that lost puppy look must be fellow freshmen. Above me, linden trees sprawl into a leafy, emerald canopy. Below me, the bricks etched with personal messages bought by annual givers and alumni tell a story of those who either walked these very paths or knew someone who had.

Stay focused. Daydreaming will not help me through college.

The Student Center, a solid fifteen-minute walk across campus, towers above the rest of the buildings; its four-stories overflow with food options, classrooms, the gym, and lush landscaping. I'll get exercise by attending class. How convenient.

My sandals snap against the Student Center's glossy tile as I wander the building searching for my classroom. Several minutes pass before I find my destination hiding in a corner of the fourth floor. My heart pounds as I run into the room buzzing with conversing students while the professor stands behind her computer. No one notices my hurried entrance. The tension in my body eases as I wipe my sweaty hands on my jeans. I was almost late for my first college class; what a great start.

But it gets better.

I walk to a seat in the front, my left side clipping the corner of a table. My book *thuds* onto the desk I've claimed. The guy sitting there turns away from his conversation, and I immediately recognize him and his posse as part of the notorious lacrosse team.

It's hard not to notice them. They travel in an unbreakable pack of gym shorts, matching team shirts, and unapologetic manliness. The guy facing me with his dark hair curling around the edge of a team cap is no different from the two teammates sitting beside him.

My face warms as I mutter, "Sorry. First class and I'm already making a scene."

He smirks and rolls his brown eyes. "I was late for my first class last year. All's good." He turns back to his teammates.

Instead of eavesdropping, I busy myself with finding my notebook, pen, and Spanish dictionary. No distractions. I'm here for an education, to ace my classes and get that diploma.

The professor clears her throat and says something in Spanish, precise and quick; she's on to the next sentence before I can mentally translate the previous one. I glance at the lacrosse players who have the same blank look on their faces. It's not just me. My understanding of Spanish is truly elementary. The placement test doesn't lie.

¡Qué lástima!

Then the professor says in English, as quickly as if she's caffeine incarnate, "For your first assignment, you will introduce yourself to the class. Say your name, where you're from, and three interesting facts about yourself. You have five minutes, and it must be memorized. Begin."

I'm writing my sentences in English to translate them when the lacrosse player clears his throat. "Hey. Already forgot my dictionary. Can I borrow yours?"

I slide it over to him without hesitation. This happened in high school every day. Someone always forgot something, and I was always prepared to lend it.

Five minutes pass, but I don't need the dictionary; short, simple sentences are what I prepared. One by one, students give their introductions. When it's my turn, I stand like everyone else, clear my throat, and speak slowly.

"My name is Melanie. I am from Missouri. I am a freshman. I am also a business major. My favorite movie is *Beauty and the Beast*."

I panicked about that last fact. No one comments after my introduction, so I sit and stare ahead, gripping the edge of my seat. I told a room full of young adults that my favorite movie is one a lot of people claim to be about Stockholm syndrome.

My first college class is going splendidly.

I sigh in relief when those fifty minutes end. Someone follows me as I escape to find my next class. I glance behind to see the same guy with curly locks, adjusting his snapback hat. He holds his hands up in defense then shoves them into his gym short pockets. "I promise I'm not following you. You headed to Math 102?" Dylan–yes, that's his name–asks as he walks beside me.

"I sure am," I say. "I was about to accuse you of stalking me. Are you a fellow Disney enthusiast and want to talk about the conspiracy of the movie *Frozen* being connected to *Tarzan*?"

"My sister begged me to see *Frozen* with her. The guys would never have let me hear the end of it."

I don't know what to say, so we quietly stroll to our math class on the "old side" of campus. It's called this for obvious reasons: the looming brick buildings, moss and ivy clinging to every surface, arched doors, and stained-glass windows create a mini replica of Hogwarts. I text Brady about it as Dylan and I enter one of the stone buildings.

We find the class without much difficulty. Dylan heads to the back of the room and says to a girl already sitting, "Thought you'd be thrilled that I am stuck with an 8 a.m. this semester."

She snorts, but I turn around and tune out their conversation as I sit in the front row, waiting for the professor to arrive. Brady would have something to say about me being friendly with an athlete who's probably popular if jocks are treated the same way here as they were in high school—like they created the universe or whatever.

A middle-aged professor runs into the room, her sunglasses almost slipping from her face. "Sorry, class. My son needed help with car stuff this morning. We will start in a few minutes."

She gets settled then hands out the syllabus, slowly reading it to us. Someone falls asleep, his own snoring waking him up. The class laughs, so she begins teaching, probably as punishment for the class's lackluster enthusiasm for her questions about how our summer went.

Math 102 is basic, and she gives us time to finish the homework assignment during class. A nagging thought won't leave me alone. This math class is easy because I didn't do well on the placement test. Good thing I must get through multiple math, economics, and finance classes to get my degree in business.

No pressure, at all.

Next on my schedule is a beginner's acting class as a fun elective. It's in the same building as my math class. It passes by without incident or anything worth noting except someone is always dying or being murdered in the improv games we play.

By eleven o'clock, the rest of the day is mine to do whatever I want with it. I haven't made friends yet, and my school job doesn't start until September to give me time to adjust to campus life. My options are to nap, read a book, go to the gym, or check out the cafes downtown for places to study.

Napping wins.

I lay in bed after lunch, studying the stark white ceiling instead of meeting and hanging out with people. Brady responds to my Hogwarts text: "You told me that after your school tour. You make any friends yet?"

How do I tell him "Of course not. I'm too awkward"?

I message Hayley and Alex, asking them about their first day. Erin belly laughs from the other side of the wall followed by Jessica's cackle. They always sound like they're enjoying college life. Sophia enters the room for a moment and promptly leaves. She's only here between classes and to sleep during weekdays.

Vague dreams find me until I twitch awake, my heart pounding as if I have been running. With clenched fists and a tightness clutching my chest, I sit up in bed with my back against the wall. My gaze drifts out the window, watching different groups of students pass by. College has started, and here I am napping and avoiding the world.

It's only the first day of class, I remind myself. No use getting worked up over something I can change. A game plan forms in my mind. I'll initiate conversations with the people I've already met; socialize during classes and not solely focus on schoolwork; I'll go to some workout classes; maybe I'll join a club or sorority. The options are endless.

But am I brave enough to embrace this new chapter in my life fully?

~ ~ ~

On Friday afternoon after classes, I head to the gym, unsure how to spend my weekend. That whole 'get friends' game plan hasn't progressed much. Any conversations with Erin and Jessica are mostly confined to our dorm bathroom; Erin's schedule at the front desk coincides with my free time and her free hours are when I do homework. Jessica is already preoccupied with sorority stuff because she's rushing this year. Friends are always surrounding Daniela.

This beloved treadmill is my companion and distraction as I watch others workout. I swallow back a lump forming in my throat. What I would do for some casual conversation about the weather or classes. I concentrate on working off the calories of those toaster pastries and granola bars I ate for breakfast this week.

My phone rings and I almost trip, a wide grin forming on my face until I realize it says "Mom" across the screen. *What could she want? Did the divorce with Dad finally go through?*

I step both feet on either side of the treadmill, press the power button, and answer, "Hello?"

"How's my college freshman?" Mom asks, the

clicking of her keyboard obvious in the background.

"Survived my first week of classes. I'm at the gym right now."

"Good for you! You can't gain that Freshman 15. Don't want to have to buy new clothes," she jokes, but I know she's serious. She made a comment to Brady after he gained a bit of weight after his first semester at college.

I glance down at my legs, no trimmer with muscle since I've been here. Quickly changing the subject, I stammer, "So, um, any reason you're calling? I mean, it's Friday, so I'm sure you have plans or something."

The typing stops. "I wanted to confirm that we were on the same page regarding your class payments."

A wave of dizziness catches me off guard, my grip tightening on the treadmill's handrail.

"Melanie, are you there?" Mom's voice brings me back to the present.

"You said keep goods grades and I'll pay for your classes," I quote her verbatim from a talk we had over the summer.

"Not good grades. Straight A's. I want you in that freshman honor's society since you couldn't make it into the honor's college."

Thanks for reminding me of my failure.

She continues. "We'll have another chat in a few months about your grades. If they aren't where they need to be, I'll cut you off." The typing resumes from her end of the phone line. "Have a good weekend. Talk to you soon."

Her conversations—brief and devastating as always.

I take several deep breaths to calm me. The threat of removing financial assistance will encourage me to keep my grades up. At least this is what I'll tell myself every time the academic pressure becomes too much.

I turn the treadmill on and hop back onto it, hoping the cardio will distract me from the stress settling over me.

I can't screw up this time.

Chapter 4

September

Two full weeks of classes have passed, and I'm surviving. The freshman experience class is a joke, accounting became another foreign language, and the only redeeming quality of psychology is the young dashing adjunct professor. Homework assignments steal much of my free time now. Taking six college courses wasn't my brightest idea; my dorm desk piled high with notebooks and textbooks is evidence of my grave error.

Have I made any friends? Erin and Jessica invited me to a few dinners with them but nothing consequential. Daniela and I make comments to each other during our class together; the awkwardness from the scavenger hunt is far behind us though Philip has reminded me several times that my illness kept our group from winning the extra credit points. I am not close to anyone, somehow. I'm too focused on my studying. The library and a cafe in town have become my second home.

Mom's threat of removing finances hangs over me

like a permanent shadow.

On a Thursday morning, I sit in accounting class, waiting to take a quiz. After fitting in extra time that morning to study, I finish the quiz sooner than the rest of the class.

I glance around the room as I hand it to the professor who grades it on the spot, a 17/20 written in red along with corrections. Maybe it's the look on my face that I can't hide, but he grabs it back from me and writes 85% at the top. *Ugh, why can't I understand simple accounting? Mom expects A's and this is not helping.*

That same evening, I sit alone in the second-floor lounge hoping the classical music blasting through my headphones will help me focus on accounting homework. Hours disappear as I read and reread the concepts, outline my notes, and triple check my homework answers. I must get this right. Failure is not on my to-do list.

I fall into bed that night thinking, *thank God tomorrow is finally Friday*.

~ ~ ~

The late afternoon clouds roam the blue skies above me while fellow students mill around the campus, planning their weekend activities. I lounge on a bench outside the dorm and sink my bare feet into the freshly cut grass below me, my sandals discarded nearby. A breeze plays with my dress's hem, a scarlet garment with spaghetti straps and the bottom flaring out in feminine pleats resting at my knees. It's one of the nicest outfits I own other than my renaissance faire costumes; I left those at home on purpose.

And it's Brady's favorite dress on me.

Butterflies swirl in my stomach at the thought of Brady; he will be here soon, park his car, and be in my arms. With Brady's fraternity being so important to him, it's been a month since I've seen him. I can't be the one who gets in the way of his "growth in leadership and friendship." These guys are an essential part of his life. If it makes him happy, then I'm happy.

But impatient to see him.

Our phone conversations grow shorter each week; my schoolwork and his fraternity activities deplete our limited time. We'll catch up this weekend. I've already made plans for us, but I'm sure Brady will find a way to modify them. First, a tour of my dorm and the campus. Then dinner and dessert at the retro diner on Main Street. And for the grand finale—a night in with buttery salted popcorn that I earned by working out at the gym today, and whatever movie we can compromise on watching.

Move aside, frat boys. It's my weekend with Brady.

But first, I wait. According to the time he said he left, he should arrive soon. In the meantime, Brady lent me his favorite book, the only book he's ever been interested in apparently. It's some fictionalized account of a Civil War battle. After going untouched, I peek it open to impress

36

him. Between paragraphs I search for his Jeep. Ten minutes pass. I keep reading and habitually scan the parking lot every minute or so. Now I don't feel so sexy in my red dress sitting alone on campus on a Friday afternoon.

He's only thirty minutes late. I shake my head, a few tears forming in my eyes as I try to justify it before I get "too dramatic" as Brady likes to call it. I got here early, and he's never on time. These emotions are from missing Brady and all the changes in my life lately. *Don't be a crybaby.*

A Jeep comes into view above the page I'm reading. I sniffle and wipe my eyes as Brady hops out, his torso-hugging plaid shirt pulling at his chest and wiry arms. The book promptly finds the ground as I sprint to him. I wrap my arms around his familiar, athletic figure radiating warmth, his musky cologne tickling my nose.

He stands rigidly while I squish his arms against him.

I speak first. "Hey! How was the drive?" I unpin him, trying to ignore the awkwardness.

He shrugs, not returning the hug or affection in any way. "It felt long. Had to stop twice."

"That's all right! You made it here safe," I say, my voice squeaking. This isn't going as I pictured it would.

Brady stares above my head, basically talking at the dorm. "Sorry for being late. I know that bugs you."

Despite my misgivings, my grin widens. I try to take

his hands, but he ignores my attempt.

I say, "It's okay. Let's grab your stuff. Finding parking is a nightmare, but you got a good—"

"Can we sit and talk for a second?" He looks at me, his lips pulled together.

Somehow unfazed by his clear lack of enthusiasm, I chatter the whole way to the bench about the weather and classes, ignoring the nerves threatening to detonate in my stomach. He gives me affirming comments. The whole time I wring my hands on my lap and wish he would say anything about it. *This clumsiness stems from being apart,* I assure myself. I grab the book as we sit down.

He begins right away. "Can we talk?"

An unnatural, high-pitched laugh escapes me. "Isn't that what we're doing?"

"Serious talk."

Squeezing the book under my fingers for good luck, I place it on the bench between us and turn toward him. What did I do wrong? Sweat gathers on my palms, and I discreetly wipe them on my dress. The last serious talk I received was Mom politely threatening me to keep good grades.

Nothing Brady could say will top that.

Brady watches the passing cars and clears his throat.

"Listen, Melanie. I need to be honest…"

What does that mean?

"…because I care about you."

You say that every time you tell me I'm being stupid. For my own good though.

"But this distance thing has been hard for me."

We've been doing this for a while.

"The fraternity has been really busy lately…"

Nothing has changed, Brady.

"…and my new internship will take me further away."

I can wait forever. We have time. We're young.

He's facing me now, those blue eyes searching mine. My heart races in response as the counter arguments in my head cease. He smiles, so I stare at my fidgeting hands.

"Always in that head of yours. Listen. It's your freshman year. Don't get so wrapped up in your studies as usual. You should enjoy these years without someone keeping you tied down."

What he's trying to say becomes clear. First Hayley and Alex left me.

Et tu, Brady?

He sighs then asks, "So, could we just be friends?"

Then fall, Melanie.

Of course, I would be making literature references when someone breaks up with me. I stiffen, realizing what's happening; it's as if I'm watching Brady and I sit next to each other on a sunny Friday afternoon through tunnel vision. He's blurring in and out of focus. I take deep breaths, trying to return to the moment.

But even my tried-and-true method is failing me.

Brady clears his throat. "I'm staying with a buddy."

I gasp for air, a strange sound somewhere between an exhalation and a squeak escaping my mouth.

"Oh, come on. It's college. You've got your whole life ahead of you. Live your best life, do all the things," Brady says as he pats my head. "I know that's not who you are, but you can learn not to be so…you." He grabs the book from the ground, the last thing tying him to me besides memories.

Brady stands and begins walking away. I should cry and beg him to stay, right? That's what they do in books. This bench is my anchor as I sink into it, numb and heavy. I blink, tears falling down my face as I spot him across the parking lot. He has the nerve to wave, climbing up into his Jeep and shutting its door. I will never forget his silly plaid shirt and my stupid red dress.

Students pass by, laughing and discussing weekend plans; birds chirp and scuttle about in the late summer heat; the sun crawls across the sky as the clouds lazily drift by absent of thought or ambition. Time passes without consequence, and I lift my body from the bench. Someone says hello as the dorm elevator carries me upward. Keys open the door's lock. I drop into the bed and remain. Even dreams are nonexistent.

I wake to darkness, my head pounding and my stomach growling. The clock tells me dinnertime has passed. I blink a few times and feel my body again, everything returning to normal, to vibrant reality.

But the only thing missing now is Brady.

~ ~ ~

Over the weekend, I descend into a murky mental abyss consisting of cookie dough ice cream, sad music that makes everything worse, and unfinished homework assignments. Sophia spends her weekends at home, so I can properly wallow. Hayley and Alex provide no help, their words well-meaning but comfortless. "You were too good for him, anyway" they tell me. They know how much I loved him.

That doesn't matter now.

Mom texts me after I update my relationship status to "single" on social media and change my profile picture to a solo one of me. I delete Brady, his frat buddies, and their partners from my friend's list.

I reply to her message: "Yeah, I'm fine. He was being distant and spent too much time with his frat." Two truths and a lie, right? She doesn't interrogate me further.

A weekend can't erase years of tying your heart around another person. Somehow, I'll untangle my life from the parts that are Brady's design. No more hiking adventures, the way he shoved me out of my comfort zone to try new activities like river floating and rock climbing. No more cheering at baseball games and celebratory meals afterwards. No more prolonged kisses after movies and car rides. No more hugs that encompassed me, reminding me I'm alive and safe. Simply, no more Brady.

Then begs the question that I'm unsure how to answer. Who am I without him? And the follow up lurking in my mind—*how did I lose myself to him?*

Chapter 5

First House Party

Everything is out of focus when I take my usual spot in math class on Monday morning. I don't fight it, letting myself sink into melancholy's vice grip. The professor is late, which allows time for brooding. *Friends text each other. I only sent Brady one message asking if he made it home okay.*

"Hey, Freshie. Pssst. Freshie with the beanie hat," a feminine voice calls behind me. Someone pokes my shoulder. I turn my head to see a redhead, her plum-painted lips parted in a smile that takes up her whole face. Normally she sits in the back with Dylan, but today they sit closer to me.

I stare in response, words refusing to form.

"Hi. Isn't your name Mackenzie? Did you do the homework?" she asks. She's never said a word to me before today. *I don't even know her name.*

I stammer, my face growing warm. "It's M-Melanie. And—uh, yes."

Well, I did half of it this time, but she'll figure that out.

She bats her eyes. "Mind if I copy it? My cat died last night—"

"You mean you were out until two o'clock in the morning," Dylan comments from behind her.

She huffs. "Not. Now. Dylan."

I clear my throat. "No, no. It's okay. You can copy it."

"Aww, thanks!" She winks with her fake eye lashes and snatches my half-complete assignment. "The name's Katrina. Call me Kat. No one likes to say my name after that hurricane, ya know?"

Kat scribbles answers as she prattles on. "Yeah, so this one here is my brother."

Looking at Kat and Dylan, I never would've guessed. I imagine her dyed hair a different color before I can see any kind of family resemblance expect in their olive skin tone and brown eyes.

Dylan interrupts my musings. "I can speak for myself, Sis. But yes. Kat is my beloved sister who can't shut her mouth."

"And I think you two would make a cute couple. Dylan spends all his time with his teammates these days."

"Kat. Stop talking already." He crosses his arms, and his jaw slightly clenches.

I'm not surprised by his reaction. We barely know each other. The extent of our interactions in Spanish class includes comments about the weather and me helping him with the answers to homework questions "he couldn't figure out". Thinking about it though, it seems like most of the homework questions are blank when he asks...

At least I'm being helpful, I guess.

Not sure why he would talk to me. Word got around our dorm that the lacrosse team hosts good parties, because they have special housing accommodations due to championship wins. The fraternity parties are supposedly noteworthy as well. I haven't been invited out. Who wants to hang out with a broken-hearted recluse trying to figure out who she is after her boyfriend dumped her?

The professor rushes into the classroom, and slams the door, breaking me from that downward spiral of thinking. Kat hasn't stopped talking the entire time, but I only catch a few words.

She winks at me. "Thanks. You're cute. Keep doing you."

My homework floats down to my desk, and I glance past Kat to find Dylan shaking his head, curly hair peeking out from under the hat that never leaves his head.

He smiles at me instead of his usual half-upturned lip. "Wait, Melanie. Here's your Spanish dictionary. Sorry for always bugging you about it."

His dimples are kinda cute, I observe as I grab the book from his outstretched hand and turn around as the professor asks for homework. But my thoughts don't linger on Dylan. I zone out the rest of my classes that morning, willing my mind to stay quiet until I can be alone.

On cue, ruminations threaten me as I aimlessly walk around campus after my final class of the day. *What is Brady doing tonight? I could text him and apologize. Why am I apologizing? He ended it with me. I don't know. If a simple sorry would allow me back into his arms, is that so bad?*

I shake away that train of thought, but only for my mind to travel to my friends back home. Our group chat has become quiet lately. Once upon a few months ago, no one could separate us. Perhaps we don't have as much in common since we aren't stuck in the same building for eight hours a day, five days a week.

I stop for a moment and discover I'm at the edge of campus near some shady trees and a convenient bench. Glancing around to make sure I'm alone, I lay down on the bench and stare up into the leaves. *Isn't this what princesses do when they're upset? They find a piece of furniture or the floor, throw themself down, and cry.*

The tears brim in my eyes until a distinct cough to my left forces me to sit up; mental breakdowns are impossible around here. I notice a figure propped against a tree, smoking what smells like weed. The smoke clears, revealing themself as a rather tall, lanky student. *So much for being alone. How did I miss him?*

He lazily smiles at me and holds his hands up as if to

surrender, a joint between his lips. He says, "Oh, no. I've been caught. Are you here to take me to campus security?"

I sniffle, straightening my bad posture. "Yes. I'm their finest spy. What gave it away?"

He wheezes, something between a cough and a laugh. "Nice one. Name's Seth. You?"

"Melanie." I recognize him from around my dorm, but is he a freshman? I haven't seen him in any classes and the way he confidently smokes an illegal substance in public gives off this jaded, uncaring upperclassman stereotype.

He lifts the joint to me. "Well, want some weed? Campus security doesn't patrol this way."

Weed. I hesitate. I've never tried it before, but it would serve as a distraction. *What if I get paranoid? What if it's not a good high? I can't embarrass myself like that to an absolute stranger.* A headache begins to form from my whirling thoughts. Seth takes a hit, completely unbothered by my silence. The smoke twists up to the trees as another wave of its distinct smell reaches me.

I shake my head. "No, thanks."

"You made a face. It too smelly for ya? Whatever. When you're ready to try it, find me. Helps take the sting off this place."

I dab my eyes with my sleeve, whether from my gloominess or the smell, I don't know.

I mutter, "Well, I better start some homework. See

47

you around."

He leans back and waves me away, taking another hit as he stares ahead. I start back toward Montgomery Hall. I can't wallow with someone else around. I don't want to throw a pity party, but what else can I do to fill the pit of loneliness in my stomach? Smoking with a stranger isn't the answer. For me, at least.

I lay in bed for another midday nap, my own way of removing the sting from this place; it never helps. Reality always returns when I wake up alone.

Honestly, I want to text Brady. I hate myself for that.

~ ~ ~

The monotony of morning classes the next day distracts me. At noon a text from an unknown number pops up on my phone as if an answer to my loneliness. I immediately tap on it.

Random Number: "Heyyy! It's Kat. Got your number from social media. You should remove that. Party tonight. Taco Tuesday. See you at 8."

The next message contains an off-campus address and a gate code. Why invite me? We interacted for five minutes yesterday. Staring at my phone screen, I shrug at the text. I'm either more optimistic today or hopeless enough to do whatever will relieve these endless negative feelings.

I text back without a second thought: "Thanks. See you later. I'll bring some cookies."

Brady told me to live my best life, right? Well, here goes nothing.

Another gym workout, a quick trip to the store for cookies, and dinner brings me to the evening hours. With shaky hands, I put on makeup and my favorite pair of jeans–they are comfortable–and a simple black T-shirt; a checkered infinity scarf completes my outfit for my first college party. *Hopefully no one notices what I'm wearing. My clothes are so outdated,* I bemoan as I hop into my car and type Kat's address into the phone's GPS. It's a sixteen-minute drive across town.

This is what it takes to make friends. I can't back out.

My stomach churns as I drive through town and into a gated neighborhood. Condos line either side of the street, their small porches and outdoor spaces decorated with furniture, trinkets, and lights. The GPS takes me in front of a skinny two-story building where I park on the empty street. Kat's condo isn't connected to the neighbor's place, and she has her own driveway.

How does she afford that, I wonder as I grab the cookies, sling my messenger bag across my body, and step toward her front porch already decorated in Halloween decor. I pause, freezing in place on the porch step. *How much do I even know about Kat?*

She's a classmate who copied my homework.

She has a brother named Dylan.

She lied about her pet dying.

49

So, nothing substantial. *This is a mistake.* I never attended parties in high school; the people who threw them never invited the student glued to her textbooks, yearbook duties, and theater commitments. Hayley, Alex, and I did our own thing—weekend nights occupied with donut runs and binging movie series. Turning on my heels, impulse calls me back to my car to spend the night surrounded by homework and more ice cream; always flight, never fight.

Yet a nagging pressure in my chest stops me in my tracks. *I may never get this chance again.* I pivot and return to the porch hoping no one saw my embarrassing reluctancy.

Breathe in, breathe out. Repeat.

Glancing around me as I knock on the door, it burst open. Kat beams in her leggings and black crop top; her makeup appears professionally done–the contouring and such I struggle to learn–while her hair is pulled into a neat, high bun. She snatches the cookies from me. My arms, like a bad habit, wrap around my torso while my hands clasp my elbows.

"Hey, it's my favorite Freshie! What's up?" Kat practically shoves me into her condo, making me trip over my high-top sneakers.

Once I find my balance, I take in my surroundings: a lofty ceiling, living room crammed with high-end furniture, a television occupying one wall, lit gas fireplace, and a massive kitchen to the side. A hallway leads somewhere beyond us, and the stairs open to a loft and more rooms. *How many rooms does one person need*, I wonder. Empty liquor bottles decorate the top of the kitchen cabinets while full bottles line the granite countertop. Meat sizzles in a gigantic pan on the gas stove.

Kat sets the cookies on the kitchen's granite island. "You can put your very large bag in my room. I lock it before every party. Can't trust anyone." She points at a room down the hallway.

"Thanks," I mutter as I venture to her room. I pass a guest bedroom and bathroom with a large stand-up shower. Her door is open, so I peek in. A king-sized bed dominates most of the space besides a petite mirror and vanity wedged into the corner. Makeup of every kind and brand crowds it; a floor-length container brimming with more cosmetics, lotions, perfumes, and the like sits next to the vanity. *Where did she get that stuff? That must have cost an actual fortune.* I drop my bag on the floor beside her bed.

"You're early, so it's only us," Kat explains when I return.

I stand by the kitchen island, unsure what to say or do. My thoughts inevitably swirl. I don't want to mess this up. Exhaling slowly, I ask, "Do you need help with anything?"

She points to a grocery bag on the counter. "Yeah. Open the plastic shot glasses and cups. Arrange it to be inviting or whatever."

I grab the enablers for tonight's drinking. Chewing the inside of my cheeks, I set everything out as directed. *Why did Kat invite me? Of everyone on campus, I would've been my last choice.*

Arranging the plastic shot glasses, cups, and the liquor bottles takes up a minute or two. Then the words leave my mouth before I can stop myself. "Okay, let me be honest." I turn to Kat. "I'm bad at small talk, I have no idea why you invited me, and I've never had a sip of alcohol except for my dad's beer."

Kat lets out a laugh that fills the room. Somehow, it shrinks my nerves.

She resumes cooking, stirring the taco meat. "Don't worry. I invited you as a thank you for letting me copy your homework. Just chill." Kat scoops the meat into a taco shell and hands it to me. "Here. You'll want a little food before you drink."

I munch on the taco while she prepares the alcoholic drink: tiny, cubed ice, tequila, and margarita mix. She doesn't hesitate even though I'm a minor.

She slides the drink over. "Drink slow. Baby sips. Don't want you tipsy before everyone gets here."

I smile and take a sip as instructed. It tastes like a slushie with a small kick to the throat.

I like it.

The initial awkwardness aside, I brave small talk. "How old are you? You have so much liquor," I comment as she makes a taco for herself.

"Twenty-two. A little behind in college. Took a year-ish off after high school. Didn't find myself."

"What're you studying?"

"Business, meaning I have no idea what I want to do. But *Nonna and Nonno* are paying, so why not?"

I nod, wondering who she referred to but refrain from asking. "Same. My mom wants me to take over the family marketing firm."

She takes a shot of tequila like it is water. "Yeah, yeah. Fun stuff. So, anyway. I gotta ask, are you single?" Kat hands me another taco then starts mass-producing margaritas.

"Um, yes actually. Recently." It's nice to say it out loud to someone who doesn't know him, someone unbiased.

"That sucks."

"It's okay. He loved his fraternity more."

"Screw him then. Was just wondering because Dylan—"

As if on command, Dylan strolls in through the front door, and I'm suddenly light-headed. His hat remains on his head, but he wears a tight gray V-neck that hints heavily at a lean, muscular figure. *Don't stare. He's a fit male in a tight shirt. Completely normal occurrence,* I think as I stare at the drink in my hand.

"Hey, Sis. Melanie," Dylan says as he grabs a beer

from the fridge then snatches the taco from Kat's hand. With a mischievous smirk, he reclines on the couch.

Kat throws her arms up. "The party has arrived!"

Dylan's middle finger responds. This gesture ignites their sibling bickering, so I sit at one of the barstools pushed against the kitchen wall, trying to disappear. The liquor and their arguing make my head spin. Gripping the edge of my seat, I think about grabbing another taco and drink. My cup is already empty.

The front door swings open and strangers enter the apartment, so I sink back into the chair and watch them. This process repeats until the condo becomes too small for the swell of bodies. My head pounds from the chorus of chattering voices and intermingling smells of cigarette smoke and weed. Kat adds to the unfolding madness by turning on music and dimming the lights; she and some other students dance along to the beat.

I understand why she lives in a standalone condo.

Someone separates from the crowd and approaches me with two full shot glasses. I blink a few times until I recognize Daniela.

She hands me one of the plastic shots. "*Hola*! I'm surprised to see you here. Are you friends with Kat?"

"Kinda? We have a class together. I let her copy my homework, so she invited me." I cringe at my honesty. I quickly follow up by asking, "How do you know her?"

"She helps coach the swim team. She does not show

up every practice but when she does, she's helpful."

"She knows a lot of people," I say.

Daniela holds the shot glass up, and I mimic. She toasts, "To Kat and her popularity."

We bottoms up the shot. I cough, some liquid dripping down my chin. Daniela stifles a laugh as Kat appears next to her. I wipe my face with my hand, unsure where to set the emptied shot glass.

Kat holds up a light orange shot bottle. "Nothing clumsier than someone's first shot. Especially straight tequila," Kat says. "Quite a rude choice. Melanie, try this whiskey. It's easy if you like cinnamon."

I hold my empty shot glass in one hand and accept the shot bottle from Kat with the other. I don't take the shot yet. I better slow down.

"Daniela, how is swimming going?" I ask, trying to distract myself from the onsetting dizziness.

She stands taller. "Practices are good. Swim meets start at the end of the month."

Kat places her hands on Daniela's shoulders. "What she didn't tell you is that she has the fastest times on the female team. Even faster than most of the guys, mind you."

Daniela swats her away. "Call me Dani. You should come to one of our local meets sometime, Melanie."

I give her a thumbs up as Kat leans into Dani and whispers something that makes her grin. Dani drops the plastic shot glass like the floor has become the trash can.

"Join us for a game." Dani says before Kat grabs her hand and pulls her away while I eye the petite bottle in my hand. I can't bring myself to down it, so I twist the lid and sip. Cinnamon kisses and burns my throat all the way down. It's not much easier to drink than tequila. *A game could be fun,* I think as I mingle with the crowd to find wherever they are playing it. Gulping against the sting in my throat, I refuse to second guess myself. Brady told me to enjoy my freshman year.

Watch me.

After more sips of the cinnamon whiskey, my mind and body start to contradict each other. What is this feeling...floating? That's the word. I'm grounded somehow, in this moment only, but my head resides in some non-existent place. My arms and legs are my anchors, but my mind and heart soar. Only this moment exists. *I can do this! I can be social without sabotaging it.*

My head bumps into someone's chest. Stumbling backwards, I behold a stunning human being holding a can of beer. He's at least six feet tall and one of the most beautiful people I've laid eyes on. It's probably the alcohol talking already. Next to him stands Seth who's wearing the same outfit I met him in yesterday. Seth winks at me in recognition. Even through my hazy mind, the smell of weed on him permeates my nose.

"I'm sorry, Sir," I say to the handsome specimen of a

man in front of me.

"Sir? Is this how freshmen are addressing upperclassmen now? I like this new rule," he replies, smooth and level-headed.

I hiccup, slightly swaying as my fingers try to find a nonexistent wall beside me. "How did you know I was a freshman?" I ask.

Sir gestures with his beer can. "Oh, I assumed because of the height."

Seth snorts at Sir's response and takes a long sip of his drink.

I need to invest in some heels.

I roll my eyes and point a finger into Sir's chest. "Well, Mister. You are correct. I may be little, but I am fierce. Don't you forget it." *Always quoting Shakespeare at inappropriate times,* I giggle to myself which finds its way out of my mouth.

He chuckles and points away from me. "Well, why don't you join us for some truth or dare since you're feeling so fierce?"

My eyes follow his finger to a small group gathered around a tower of wooden blocks including Kat, Dani, Dylan, and one of the lacrosse players from Spanish class named Isaac. I lead them over to the game, my original goal, when I notice truth or dare challenges etched on the wooden blocks. How grownup. I sit on the couch between Kat and Dylan to keep them from bickering. Kat offers Sir and Seth a shot.

Sir waves it away. "I have an internship interview tomorrow morning. Can't be hungover for it."

Seth grabs the shot and guzzles it while Kat shoots back the other one.

I zone out until it's my turn. My first block asks me to remove a piece of clothing, so I untie and fling my shoes to the ground. When it's his turn, the stunning upperclassman whose name I haven't heard yet picks a block that instructs him to tell his funniest drunk story; the block tower slowly falls to the living room table.

He folds his hands in front of him. "I was a sophomore. My buddies and I went to Main. Woke up the next morning with my head at the foot of the bed, in my underwear. The one friend who remembered said we went for a highway drive, and I puked out the window while we drove. All the way down the highway at eighty miles per hour. Didn't get arrested."

The group bursts into cackles and snorts. I gaze at him a little too long, and he raises his eyebrows at me. To distract myself, I restack the blocks as the hysteria begins. Dylan arm wrestles with Kat who loses, so she takes a shot. Kat takes off her shirt for her dare, the host chilling at her own party in a bralette. How grownup. Seth and Isaac switch their shirts. Why so many blocks about clothing? Dani mixes and drinks uncomplimentary liquor and almost throws it up. Staring contests. More stories.

Singing. Dancing. More shots. I can't keep track anymore.

Dylan grabs a block and reads, "Everyone turns around, and you judge who has the best butt. Winner takes a shot." We laugh as each person twirls to flaunt their behind. Someone even twerks.

With too much certainty Dylan announces, "Melanie." I remember this with clarity because no one ever picks me out of a group like that. Other players laugh while Seth makes a noise of agreement. I obediently take the shot I'm given.

Beyond that moment, my memory fails me. That's a drinking cliche; you get drunk and don't remember. But that's how it happens. I recall snapshots: movement, laughter, singing, music, smoke, coughing, warmth, cologne, perfume, sweat...

Then nothing at all.

Chapter 6

It's dark and silent. *Where am—oh. I'm in Kat's apartment,* I remember. My stomach churns, forcing me to wake up. *Not good.* Stumbling from the couch through the pitch-black room, I drop to the guest bathroom floor and hurl into the toilet. A coughing fit follows profuse sweating and the resume of my usual rapid heartbeat. The liquor's aftermath cruelly leaves me miserable and cold on the bathroom floor.

Time passes–who knows how long I lay on the ground–until I manage to crawl back to the couch, where a fitful sleep swoops me away from reality. Beams of sunlight from open blinds wake me up sometime later. I sit up to survey my surroundings, and my heart drops. Kat's microwave clock reads "11:00". I missed my classes. *Here you go again messing things up,* I chide myself as an exasperated sigh escapes my mouth. Some of these classes incorporate participation points and not showing up will worsen my grades.

I take a few deep breaths before I freak out in front

of my new friends. *Don't ruin this too soon.*

The sound of a gurgling coffee machine and sizzling bacon makes me peek my eyes open. In the kitchen Kat and Dani wade through the aftermath of the party. A throbbing headache splits my head. I moan and collapse back into the cushions, curling into a ball.

Kat sets a bowl of cereal, strips of bacon, and a brimming mug on the coffee table in front of me.

"Your first hangover is always the worst...actually, no. They all suck." She laughs.

"Thanks," I grumble as I straighten and grab the steaming mug. My stomach constricts at the coffee's bitter aroma, but I take a sip; the words "AP Scholar" peek out from under my fingertips. *That's odd. I have the same mug.* This mug means she did excellent on several AP tests in high school, but Kat doesn't seem like the type interested in academics. Her endless commentary about last night and a fresh wave of nausea stops me from speculating how she earned the mug.

"Well, that party was lit," Kat concludes as she cleans food and drink debris.

Dani adds, "I didn't know you were so talkative, Melanie."

I shrug, focused more on trying to eat than explaining myself.

Kat rolls her eyes. "Once you're comfortable, you're fine. Last night proved that. Have some confidence in yourself. Sheesh."

But it took alcohol to do that, I reflect as I watch Kat throw away emptied liquor bottles and plastic shots; the trash can is chockfull of evidence from last night's scene. The sight makes me want to throw up.

I swallow another swig of coffee before speaking. "So, did Dylan and I—did we do anything more than casual?" I ask, my memory blurry after a couple rounds of truth or dare.

Kat raises her eyebrows. "You mean, you don't remember?"

Oh, no. What did we do? I'm already blushing.

She gives a long pause. Kat and Dani burst into laughter. When they are done, it's Kat who speaks. "You only exchanged phone numbers. But he voted you 'best butt'. Congrats on that achievement."

I grimace, fuzzy memories emerging to the surface: Sir laughing at some joke I made; Seth offering me a joint; Dani spilling her drink over the wooden blocks. *See, I remembered something*, I congratulate myself even though I blacked out at my first college party.

"I missed morning practice, so I'll go now. Thanks for the party, Kat! See you around, Melanie," Dani says as her teammates pull into the driveway and honk the car's horn.

"Good luck living in that dorm. Stay out of her way, and you'll be fine!" Kat calls to Dani as the front door shuts. My headache keeps me from wondering what Kat meant by these words.

I finish my food and coffee in silence. With the AP Scholar mug in my hand I comment, "So, you're secretly a genius?" I hold up the mug to her before I put it in the dishwasher.

She scoffs. "Nah. I stole it from Dylan. Smart boy, especially at math. He worked hard in high school and all he has to show for it were good grades and that stupid mug. Don't expect much from him."

"How is he in our math class? It's one class away from the most basic math class they offer at the college."

"Last year he randomly filled in the bubbles on the placement test to see which class he would place in. Lowest one, shocker. And now he's in class with us."

I fill the dishwasher with dirty dishes and let my thoughts drift about the smart guy who doesn't try anymore. *What happened to him,* I wonder as I grab my bag from Kat's room and collect my shoes and phone.

"Thanks for a fun party," I say as I open the front door and wave.

She yells as I'm closing it, "Get yourself a fake ID. We could live it up at the bars!"

I grin at her idea.

The drive back to school is the perfect time for me to reflect. Campus already looks different in my eyes. The sprawling columns, brick buildings and walkways, and manicured landscape haven't changed. Campus feels more like home; all it took was being invited to a party, new friends, and a little bit of alcohol.

Okay. A lot of alcohol.

A pesky headache confines me to my room until dinnertime. Dinners are dreadful here. Between the greasy food, limited meal options, and having no excuses for why I sit alone most days, I have come to loathe dinnertime. Regardless, that evening I wait in zigzagging lines of people spanning the entire dining hall then find an empty table to eat soggy chicken on a bed of iceberg lettuce.

To my surprise, Sir and Seth walk toward my table not long after I sit down.

"Good evening, Miss Melanie," Sir says as he and Seth sit across from me. "Saw you in line and thought you could use some company."

Okay. Small talk. You got this. Go.

"Hey, guys! I think I know you too well after last night. Except. I don't think I caught your name," I say to Sir. *Smooth transition and not obvious. Nicely done for once,* I congratulate myself.

Sir's grin widens, the skin around his eyes crinkling. "It's Harrison."

"Are you friends with Kat?"

"She and I went to high school together. Same country clubs too." He pauses and sets a hand on Seth's shoulder. "Seth here is my protégé since we're getting finance degrees. Well, my future business partner. We're juniors."

Country clubs? That sounds fancy. *So why are Kat and Harrison talking to a freshman like me? They are in a totally different league.*

Seth swirls the spaghetti on his plate. "Yeah, yeah. We're gonna be like the next *Wolf of Wall Street* without the illegal stuff. Seen that movie, right? I'll be able to sell anyone a pen after this degree."

Harrison fist bumps with Seth and asks me, "What are you studying?"

"Business. Nothing fancy."

"You can join us when we take over the stock market."

Seth sighs, rubbing his temples. "Someday, but not today. The only thing that matters is this hangover won't go away."

Harrison shakes his head. "The boys at the house don't understand the meaning of quiet."

Don't tell me they are in a fraternity. This is exactly who I don't want to be mixed up with. *Brady was one guy. Doesn't mean they're all dirtbags,* I reassure myself. Can't judge or I'll never make friends.

I clear my throat, wringing my hands under the table. "Sooo…are you in a frat?"

"You're looking the president of [Greek letters]. And Seth here is a new pledge." Harrison puffs out his chest.

"I finally gave in and pledged. Figured it would look good on a resume," Seth mutters.

"You okay, Melanie? You're making a face," Harrison comments.

Seth adds, "Someone hasn't learned how to hide their emotions."

I hold my hands up. "Okay, I have nothing against your fraternity. But my ex was unofficially married to his frat brothers."

"Oh, we are a brotherhood, but don't worry," Harrison defends. "We make time for others outside the frat."

I smile. "Well, good. I want to hang out sometime!"

Where did that come from? Me hanging out with two older fraternity guys? I must be desperate.

A horde of fellow fraternity boys swoop in, filling up the entire circular table. More guys to distract me from the one I think about every day. I pick at my food as they chatter about some upcoming Greek life event that weekend; I don't have anything to add to this conversation.

I excuse myself after finishing my salad, but as I walk away from the table, Harrison calls out, "Hold on, Miss Melanie." He catches up to me. "If you want to hang out with us, well, I have a guy who can get you a solid fake ID for cheap. Like sixty bucks. And it's ready in a week or less."

"Perfect timing. Kat mentioned wanting to hang out at the bars too."

"Yeah. Be careful who you tell about the fake ID. Don't want that info getting to your Resident Director, Nikki. She'll have you reported to the housing department so fast."

Nikki seems nice from what Taylor and Erin said about her. Maybe she's a stickler for campus rules.

Harrison continues. "I dub you an honorary sister. You could rush this fall too. Recruitment starts soon."

"I'll consider it."

"Perfect. Also, can I get your number? We can set up a time for some accounting tutoring. You. Shall. Pass."

I mentioned struggling in accounting last night at the party. Great. I hand him my phone, and he types in his number.

He hands the phone back. "See you around!" He waves and returns to the table teeming with frat boys.

With that successful interaction brightening my mood, I return to my room to do homework. Underage drinking—the most illegal thing I've ever done. Add an impending fake ID to my growing criminal record too. This university is slowly corrupting me, and I don't care.

Because I have friends now.

Chapter 7

Monday rolls around, and college life has fallen into a monotonous pattern of classes, workouts, and homework with rushed meals filling any gaps in my available waking hours; that fake ID can't come soon enough. I need a social outlet, but Kat and her posse spend their time at the bars. Harrison promised the ID should be done by Thursday.

Change is already coming for my schedule though; today is my first shift at the school's Work and Learn program as an "Administrative Assistant". Extra cash and a chance to build my resume? I couldn't say no to the admissions counselor convincing me to sign up for it.

Another addition to my ever-growing to do list. I make great decisions.

After classes I walk to the admissions building and ask the front desk worker where to go. She points to the stairs, and I descend into the basement to find a miniature room like the builder's afterthought. A rectangular table almost bigger than the room, ten or so young adults, and laptop cords choking the tile floor greet me. Carefully stepping over the cords and backpacks, I sit in the only available seat around the table.

For work duties, I complete whatever is assigned to me on the cleaning list then wait for an administrative task or project from a counselor. I rest my head on the table, my posture for the next four hours unless I get assigned to do something. I'm exhausted and don't want to think about homework. That's what tonight is for.

"Are you as bored as I am?" someone to my left asks. I glance over at a guy wearing a shirt that's too professional for this setting: a button up with a black clip on tie and an expression that I'm sure mirrors my own.

I yawn. "It's only week one, too."

He shakes his head. "I cleaned the doors today, and it took five minutes."

"Try mopping. This whole place is basically carpet."

"That's brutal." He holds out his hand. "Andre. Freshman and future lawyer. I think we live in the same dorm."

I shake his hand. "Melanie. Freshman and future owner of my mom's marketing firm. I can confirm that I've seen you around the same dorm."

He smiles. "Well, CEO Melanie, we will survive this together."

"The Admission's Sweatshop will not be our undoing." I immediately wince. *Oh no. Was that insensitive?*

I can't be making jokes like that to people I've just met. Dumb move.

He chuckles, loud but personal; his laugh is meant for me and no one else. He wipes his eyes and says, "Well, want to watch a movie?" He holds up one of his earbuds to me as he opens his laptop. "Might help with the boredom."

I take the earbud, and we watch some mindless but clean comedy movie. The movie ends sooner than the shift. Andre shuts the laptop, and I give him the earbud.

He yawns and slides his laptop into its bag. "Somehow, we still have time to kill. So, what brings you here to this campus?"

"I'm supposed to tell you it's because of the prestigious business school, right?"

"Of course. I'm reporting these answers back to the counselors."

I laugh. "I hail from the beloved state of Missouri, but this school was Mom's alma mater. Admissions people love that. And yes, because of the supposed good business school."

"Makes sense. My dad pastors a small church in a town over and Ma stays home with my three younger sisters. I didn't want to go too far away."

He's a pastor's kid, huh? I tuck that information away in my head.

"You have an opinion about that. Can't hide it when

it's all over your face." His smile lightens his whole face, his cheeks rising under his glasses. "It's okay. No offense taken."

How am I already messing this up? I clasp my hands in my lap. "No, wait. Uhh, let me explain. There's nothing wrong with you or your dad. I went to a private school. Bunch of so-called Christians who didn't follow the rules they said they believed in."

Shouldn't take a religion to be a kind and decent human being but whatever. I keep this to myself. It feels like gossip, and I'm not sure Andre will appreciate it. I roll my eyes at the thought of my previous classmates.

He raises his eyebrows. "Makes sense. Not representing Jesus like they should. What a shame." He turns to face me. "Do you believe in God?"

My eyes widen. "That's a pretty deep question to ask a stranger."

He shrugs, his grin unwavering. "Well, we'll be together a lot."

I hesitate for a moment but decide to indulge him. "Haha. Fine. If God exists, he's distant at best."

"I can understand your view on that..."

I quickly change the subject. "So, you're the man of the house. Are you surviving that excess of estrogen?"

"I love my sisters. And I'll be the first in my family to get a college degree too. Well, outside of ministry, that is."

"That's awesome! Good for you."

An alarm blares from his phone, and I jump in my seat. He stands and stretches his arms. "Well, we've survived our first shift. We'll compare work schedules next time I see you. I need to get home for Ma's birthday," he says.

I grab my backpack from under the table and swing it over my shoulder. "Sounds like a plan! Nice to meet you." We triumphantly escape the building and go our sperate ways as I head to the gym before dinner.

I smile as I run on the treadmill, a warm feeling settling in my chest despite my heart threatening to break out of it from the cardio. I have a work friend! I need that fake ID then I'll be on my way to happier days at university.

~ ~ ~

A headache pounds my head as I trudge to work on Wednesday afternoon. Another Taco Tuesday in the books and another hangover for me. Hopefully Andre won't notice. At work Andre and I compare our working schedules and to our relief, we share similar shifts on Mondays, Wednesdays, and Fridays.

"At least we have each other for three shifts," Andre comments as we sit at the table for another "workday".

He grabs out his laptop, so I pull my things closer to me to make enough room for him and the other students crowded around the table.

"We got twenty hours every week here. Do you think

we will ever do anything other than cleaning?" I ask him.

"I'll be able to start my own cleaning business after this," Andre replies as he opens his laptop. "And you can be the CEO if you want."

I laugh then mimic him, staring at my own laptop screen where an unfinished psychology paper mocks me. With a looming due date, aka tomorrow, I put in my headphones and continue to search for relevant research articles about my topic on the increase of anxiety and depression in adolescents.

Not long into researching, my phone vibrates with a message. I slide my finger on the screen to find a text from Harrison: "You, me, and your accounting homework tonight."

Harrison knows what he's talking about for introductory accounting, so hopefully the tutoring goes well. My heart beats faster at the realization—this would be the first time we would be alone together. What about a driven, handsome man has me so bothered?

At 5:00 I electronically submit my psychology paper through the school's online portal and gather my things. Andre and I part ways—him to his house to get ready for Wednesday night church service and me to eat dinner alone at the deli on campus.

I stop by the dorm to change into comfy clothes then drive to Harrison's frat house; the buildings are technically off-campus, so they don't get in trouble for the partying.

I park along the street and stare up at the mansions before me. They appear the same; the Greek names are just Greek to me.

People pour in and out of each house because it's rush week for the fraternities and sororities. *I'll rush next semester. Already got too much going on,* I think as I wander the sidewalk, studying each house's Greek letters engraved into the building. Being in a sorority will be a good addition to my resume, and I can make some friends too.

Harrison smokes a cigarette near the entrance of a house. When he sees me, he drops the cigarette into the receptacle and waves me inside with him. Colossal white columns hold everything in place while several banners boast Greek letters. We pass a room that has a pool table and mini fridges; another large room contains a platform and tables without chairs, the perfect place for a party. Past the common areas are winding hallways and endless doors. I wonder about the stories and secrets brewing and lurking behind every closed one.

Harrison's room reeks of weed and whatever cologne he unsuccessfully used to cover the stench. He excuses himself to the bathroom, so I examine a small bookshelf lined with business and finance books.

Seth bursts into the room without knocking, and I startle. He eyes me up and down then glances around the room. Does it look suspicious that I'm here? Hopefully the accounting book I'm holding makes it clear this meeting is for studying purposes only.

"Where's Harrison?" Seth asks.

Harrison peeks his head out of the bathroom. "What's up?"

"You got that business paper for me?"

"Only if you have the money." Harrison moves to his desk, shuffling through different stacks of papers.

Seth's hands comb through his pockets, and he retrieves the money. They exchange cash for a homework assignment. Harrison tucks the money into his wallet, and Seth clutches a paper not written by him. Seth nudges me with his shoulder before leaving. I stare at the accounting book in my hands, unsure what to say, if I should say anything. I'm sure people do this often, right?

But why does Harrison need the money if he's rich? Why risk getting in trouble?

Unabated by the unethical exchange, Harrison motions for me to sit on the blue futon while he searches for the homework that I gave him to check over. I sit down and set my accounting book on the coffee table in front of me as he pushes his weed bowl aside and joins me on the futon.

Harrison cracks his knuckles. "Okay, Miss Melanie. Let's go over this homework."

For the next hour, he explains my mistakes—which are plenty—before helping me through the basic accounting formulas. Just what I need more of—math. This is hopeless.

"I give up," I say, slamming the book closed. "This quiz tomorrow will suck if I study or not."

He laughs. "If you need some motivation, I have prescription pills I can sell you for concentration and energy. I only use them when I need to pull an all-nighter."

"I'll let you know if I need them. I have to pass accounting though."

"Good thing I need volunteer hours for the fraternity. We'll need weekly sessions for a bit."

"You're so encouraging." I lightly punch his shoulder. He playfully rolls his eyes, and I wonder about the charm some possess; charm that I clearly lack. Everything about Harrison is likable, even the stereotypical corduroy pants, blue button-down shirt, and shiny watch. I wonder if he knows about his superpower, his charisma that draws everyone to him.

I stretch, yawning and shoving my homework into the book, ready to change the subject. "So, have any formals coming up?"

He runs his fingers through his hair. "Yes, we have one in a few weeks so that the new people can enjoy their first formal as members."

"Who are you taking?" I swallow the lump in my throat, resisting the urge to fidget with my fingers or pick at my nails.

I'm not subtle at all.

Harrison shoots up, pacing the room. "Okay. Her name is Lauren. She's in…" My attention trails off as he lists some Greek letters.

I lean back onto the couch, trying to be more casual. "So what? Ask her then."

"She's been on and off with some lacrosse player for a while. Don't want to get involved with that situationship."

Who is she dating on the team?

I focus back onto Harrison and watch as a grin spreads across his face. He clearly doesn't see me as anything but his struggling pupil. I exhale, the tension in my body fading.

I shrug. "Well, she might officially break up with him and you can make your move."

His eyes find mine, and he nods. "You're right. I won't give up on her. Not yet."

How heroic. Humans always fight for the person they can't have. Hopefully he didn't notice my interest, and we can brush this off as the freshman who tried and failed to get noticed by a junior.

A text message on my phone saves me from more of this conversation.

Kat: "Thirsty Thursday tomorrow?"

"Hey, did my ID come in?" I ask Harrison.

He grabs an envelope from his desk, and a devious smile rises to his lips.

I text Kat back: "Fake ID is in. You busy tonight?"

Her reply takes two seconds: "Duck yeah. My house at 8."

I love when people don't proofread texts.

I grab my wallet from my bag, handing Harrison the money as he places the envelope in my hands. "Do you want to go out with us tonight?" I ask.

He grabs a pill bottle from his desk. "I have an important exam tomorrow." He pops the white pills into his mouth, swallowing like it's nothing. "And remember you have a quiz too. Don't stay out too late." His smirk says everything he doesn't.

He knows I'll be out all night.

I leave the frat house without drawing out my goodbye. I've been embarrassing enough tonight with my clear lack of understanding of basic accounting principles and my straightforwardness.

Why do I care about some nicely clothed frat guy who's smart and driven? Questions bombard me all the way to my dorm until the realization finally hits me. *He reminds me of Brady*, I acknowledge as I walk up the stairs to my room. Harrison is a copy of the guy I think about every day.

Ruminations about going out tonight soon crowd out my thoughts about charismatic frat boys I can't have. Standing in front of my closet, another dilemma unfolds—my clothes are outdated. One by one, I slide the hangers to examine my shirts, but nothing is mature enough for the bars. I peek at Sophia's open closet door. She's skinnier than me, and she's not here.

An idea pops into my head. I walk through the bathroom and knock on the door to Erin and Jessica's room. Jessica is taller than me but seems close to the same size in clothing.

Erin opens the bathroom door, her eyes lighting up. "Oh, hi! What brings you to our humble abode?"

"Is Jessica here? I need to borrow some clothing. Going out tonight and my clothes are too…"

"Comfortable?"

"Yeah, T-shirts and jeans won't cut it out there. The bouncers will see through my fake ID."

Jessica appears at Erin's side and assesses me, scowling at my sweatpants and high school theater T-shirt. *I should have worn something cuter to see Harrison*, I reflect as Jessica spins and opens her closest teeming with clothes and accessories.

She sighs as she runs her fingers over different tops. "I see your predicament. This might be my toughest case other than Erin here who I've given up on. But I have just the outfit for you."

Jessica gestures me over to her closet and grabs out a black and white striped tank top. It reminds me of a sports referee, but if this is what the kids wear these days, I won't argue. Handing me the tank, she searches for bottoms to complete my outfit. She finds some sleek but stretchy black shorts from her dresser drawers and a small purse clutch with a strap.

"You're a little wider in the hips and thighs than me, so these shorts will work. Oh, let me fix your hair too! It would be cute with some defined curls."

Jessica grabs my hand, pulling me into the bathroom. My lips form the words "help me", and Erin's laugh echoes in the bathroom as she places a chair from their room in front of the mirror. We chat about classes and how Jessica is rushing for several sororities, nothing story-worthy. Jessica brushes out my wavy hair while waiting for the curling iron to heat up; this act brings me back to the moment and what I am about to do. My thoughts pull me further away from the conversation as the small talk continues between my suitemates.

I stare at myself in the bathroom mirror, then try to relax my face with little success; the bars' bouncers will catch a scared college freshman if my facial expressions give me away. Nonchalance—the only way I'll convince anyone that I belong on Main Street with everyone else. Not legally, but how else can I hang out with Kat and her friends more often? It's the bars and clubs where they gather. So, I'll do the same.

Jessica must sense my fear or see my knees bouncing. She places her hands on my shoulders and gives a gentle squeeze. "Lots of freshmen do this. Your ID will work. Might even see me out sometime. After rush week of course."

I glance at Erin for extra support.

"You look great! Please be safe," she says. I wonder if she goes to the bars or not. What does she do for fun around here?

"Keep your drink with you, okay?" Jessica warns as she grabs my hair for the first curl.

I can do this. Everyone does this.

Breathe in, breathe out. Repeat.

Chapter 8

First Night At The Bars

9 o'clock that same night finds me at Kat's apartment with Dani, another swimming teammate, some friend of Kat's, and a text from Dylan to Kat promising that we could meet up with him and a few of his teammates. We down a shot or two before the bars will welcome our buzzed bodies. Kat invited some guy–I've forgotten his name and am too embarrassed to ask again–who drives us to Main Street in Kat's car; he's our designated driver tonight. Surely two shots aren't dangerous to the blood alcohol level.

Maybe it's his speedy driving or my nerves, but my stomach twists into familiar pains; I might puke before we arrive. *Will I be able to get in with my fake ID? What will the bars be like? What if I'm separated from the group? What if they leave me behind at the end of the night?* I lean my head against the car window, my forced deep breathing leaving condensation behind.

I can trust Kat. She invited me out with her, I remind

myself despite my racing pulse. She knows it's my first night with my fake ID. Kat won't ditch me in the bar or leave Main without me, surely.

Our driver slows the vehicle as we travel along the cobblestone roads splattered with strobing LED lights, antique streetlamps lit with flames, and passing cars' headlights brighten up the night. Staring out the car window, I take in the buildings containing blaring noises and movement within their fragile and aging construction. My wide eyes watch the horse carriages move alongside vehicles. The longer I focus on this moment, the more Main Street is a contradiction, a mix of modern and old-timey vibes.

He parks before my stomach can betray me, and we step onto the infamous Main Street. Bars dominate every corner. Droves of people carelessly cross the street. Car horns, shouting, laughter, and music fill my ears. Men loiter against walls and in patio chairs as they smoke and soak in the view: countless body shapes, skin, and high heels. Kat leads our group along the sidewalk, linking her and my arms together as we strut on the uneven concrete.

Kat leans closer to me. "Did you see that guy? His eyes bugged out when you walked by. My little Freshie already getting attention."

A low whistle sounds from a patron to my right, and I grimace. These men don't even know me. They see my outer shell that they have reduced to an object. *This is just how the world is,* I remind myself as I discreetly pull at my short's hem that has been slowly creeping upward. I focus ahead of me, ignoring any further stares or whistles. I won't let it ruin my night.

Our first stop is Tommy's Place. Kat pushes me in front of her, and I grab the fake ID that is surely burning a hole in my borrowed clutch. My hands shake as I hand the bouncer my forged card. *Do I look like I'm from Alabama? Should I fake a southern accent or remain silent? Does the name Clarissa suit me?* He haphazardly checks my ID and waves me inside. A sigh of relief escapes my lips.

Inside reveals a sports bar lacking lights and proper seating. Kat charges past me and disappears into the crowd. I stand in the middle of the bar, squinting at the dim lights as people bump into me. Smoke swirls right in my line of vision, but I catch Kat's hand waving over the swell of people much taller than me. I squirm past the other patrons and stand around the table that Kat secured for us.

I shift from foot to foot, wishing for a chair and continue to take in everything around me. Will I see anyone from my classes? What if I see Andre? *Can't expect perfection from anyone, not even a Pastor's kid,* I laugh to myself.

"Tonight's on me!" Kat yells, pulling me from my thoughts as she proceeds to order at the bar. She soon returns with plastic cups brimming with blue liquid and hands them to each of us.

"Here's your first double shot, Melanie!" Kat cheers.

I roll my eyes. "I can't even do one without spilling it."

"Let me help you," Dani says. I hand her the cup, and she holds it as I guzzle the concoction of mystery booze and what tastes like an energy drink. Some of the liquid drips down my chin. Heat rises in my cheeks. Dani clears her throat, holding back a chuckle while Kat snorts at my clumsiness.

Already making a fool of myself, I lament as I watch the group expertly down their double shots and toss their cups to the table. A waitress appears as if on demand, scoops up the emptied cups, and sets down a bucket full of liquor and new cups.

Dani glances down and shakes her head at the amber liquid. "Long island tea? How basic, Kat."

Kat sticks out her tongue as she pours from the bucket into our cups. As she fills my cup, the drink overflows and splashes into the table, but she makes no move to clean it up.

Kat huffs. "You mean 'thanks for paying the tab and providing me a way to get through the evening', right?" She cheers with everyone and takes a long sip.

I lean over to Dani. "Is that really tea?"

Dani holds up her drink. "Find out yourself."

I drink the iced booze, and it goes down smoothly.

Too smoothly. Well, whatever that is, it's not tea. I like alcohol better this way, the subtly of it.

A specific song starts playing, and Kat throws her hands up and sprints to the dance floor. Leaving our half-empty bucket behind, our group joins the growing mania around us. The liquor licks my veins, lighting a flicker of confidence as I join the crowd.

On the sad excuse of a dance floor, Kat performs the dance steps to the music along with other patrons. Unsure what to do with my own body, I sway, forced to the edge of the dance floor by flailing arms and coordinated feet. The song ends but that doesn't stop the frenzy; soon the crowd mingles into one large mass, some nonsensically moving while others dance on each other.

I lean against the wall, avoiding being stepped on. Someone from the crowd approaches me. I think he's from my orientation class, but I've never spoken to him before. He obviously recognizes me, so I politely wave.

"Not sure if you remember me but I'm…your phone number…we could eat…" is all I hear him say between the base and the beat.

He holds his phone out to me, the screen to input my contact info open. How do I say no? Can I shake my head and walk away? My sweaty hands reluctantly type in my name and a made-up cell number, and I hand his phone back to him. He flashes his teeth and pumps his fist to the music. Moving closer to me, his drink sloshes over its sides. I step out of the way before the liquor splashes on me.

A knot ties in my stomach despite the alcohol coursing through my body. I glance around, looking for an excuse to leave, but Kat and Dani disappeared amongst the bodies, sounds, and darkness.

My classmate leans over me, his breath saturated with liquor and cigarette smoke. "Want me to get you a drink?"

The wall digs into my back, and I agree to the drink request even as Jessica's warning of drinks from strangers echoes in my brain. I want to get out of here. He disappears to the bar, so I retreat to the bathroom. With only two toilets, I wait in line as others compete for the mirror, fixing their makeup and hair and adjusting clothing.

When it's my turn, I stand in the stall and breathe deeply instead of doing my business. *He wasn't doing anything suspicious. He wanted to hang out with you. Get to know you,* I assure myself, trying to soothe my heart knocking against my chest. I wipe my palms on my shorts, deciding to use the bathroom. *I need to buy a few more minutes, so he'll forget about me.*

Someone knocks on the two stalls. "Got coke in the back if anyone wants to have some real fun," a female voice beckons, and several women leave the bathroom, the door *swooshing* closed.

Does she mean...oh, not soda. *I'll stick to drinks tonight,* I decide as I try to zip my shorts. The zipper slides into my hand. *Of course, my zipper would break on my first night out.* Another patron vigorously knocks on the bathroom door.

I slip out, holding my hands in front my shorts, and mutter "sorry" as I wash my hands. Standing in front of the mirror, I wonder what to do about the clothing dilemma. It should be a simple fix, but I stay frozen, unable to think clearly.

"It's more common than you think," a brunette to my right comments. "Here. Let me help you." She folds my shorts, pulls a bobby pin from her long hair, and slides the pin to hold the folded cloth in place. She tucks in my shirt and adjusts it to make the folds and pin discreet. My shorts are even shorter but at least my underwear remains hidden.

"Thank you," I say as I examine my outfit in the mirror.

She fixes her ponytail and finishes reapplying her lip gloss, smacking her lips together. "No problem. Us girls gotta stick together. Cute hair by the way."

The woman next to her adds, "Yeah, the outfit extenuates your figure. Go out and flaunt that little body of yours."

Need affirmation or encouragement? Go to any bars women's bathroom, apparently. Everything about the exchange makes me smile.

I must face the music sometime. After taking deep breaths, I emerge from the bathroom, but I don't see my classmate or anyone else from our group either. Panic rises in my stomach and grips my throat again. I don't want to be alone here. *God, if you're there, help me find someone I know.*

As if an answer to my prayer, I spy Dylan across the room standing at a table surrounded by empty cups, a liquor bucket, and a single beer. I wave at him and dodge people as I approach his table. Ease sweeps over me—a familiar face in a sea of strangers.

"Finally. Someone I know," I say as I join him at the table that, sadly, has no seats either.

His signature smirk appears on his face. "Congrats on breaking the law like your peers."

I roll my eyes. "You're illegal too."

He sips his beer then shrugs. "Not too much longer."

"Whatever. Where's your teammates?" I don't recall seeing Dylan alone before at school or Kat's house parties.

"Doing what they do best. Destroying their livers and finding someone to sleep with."

"Wow. Jealous much?"

He looks out over the bar, his eyes staring at nothing, seemingly far away from this moment. He eventually answers, "Nah. Just a beer and a full night of sleep for me."

"Well, why don't you get this newbie a proper beer?"

He waves a waitress over and requests two beers. She reappears a few minutes later with the bottles.

I hold mine up in the air and say, "Cheers to a full night of blissful sleep." He taps his bottle to mine, and we drink. The beer feels less like something trying to kill my insides and more like a typical drink with a subtle citrus aftertaste. *Not a bad choice of drink, Dylan.*

We stay here, side-by-side but not touching. Conversation is minimal, but I don't mind. We watch the push and pull, the ebb and flow of the crowd mingling around us. The pounding music and dim lights are my only tie to reality.

Kat finds us sometime later, her legs wobbling as she braces herself with the table. "Our favorite beer drinker has found a buddy. How precious."

"I'm surprised you're standing," Dylan shoots back.

Kat winks. "The night is still young. Going over to the club across the street. You coming?"

He shakes his head. "I'm the designated driver tonight."

"You mean like every night?" Kat pats his face then grabs my hand. I wave at Dylan as she pulls me to the door along with Dani and others I don't know, our own designated driver in sight.

We hop across the street to a club called 24/7. How creative. I have another drink or two. Back and forth, between the sports bar and effervescent dance floor. Kat falls several times. Dani throws up in the bushes. Movement keeps me grounded in the moment while reality swirls around me. The night blurs between the bar and the club.

Anywhere we are, I look for Dylan and that silly smirk of his. I don't know why.

~ ~ ~

Kat pulls her car up to the front of my dorm, the tire bumping into the curb. The stereo's booming music follows me inside. Fumbling at the elevator's two buttons, I spot Erin at the check-in desk with Andre; they speak in low voices, so I can't hear what they say. I turn to face them, and my whole world spins. *Are my eyes flipping around inside my head? Because that's what it feels like right now.*

I'm definitely tipsy.

"Heeey, guys!" I stumble toward them, drawing out my words because it's hilarious. I am a funny, awesome person.

"Well, look who it is. It's CEO Melanie herself." Andre exclaims, still wearing his nice jeans and a dress shirt from work earlier today. Erin waves at me but won't look me in the eye.

I lean against the convenient couch across from the desk. "It's sooo late. Erin, my dearest friend, your work shift is over. You should be out there living your best life!"

I always make sure everyone hears Brady's final wish for me. They will thank me later. I'm a good person. Everyone should like me. I'm so friendly. Did I mention I'm awesome?

Erin puts away her laptop and homework, ignoring my drunken wisdom. A wave of dizziness gracelessly pulls me down onto the couch, and I drop my purse clutch that I somehow didn't lose tonight. I fumble with the cushions, trying to find my feet again. Andre laughs, averting his eyes from my rolled shorts that are slowly coming undone in the front where the zipper used to be. I lost the zipper, I guess.

Andre says, "Okay, Melanie. I'm walking you to your room. We'll talk later, Erin. Keep your chin up and get some sleep."

He gently pulls me up, hands me my clutch, and guides me to the elevator. Real gentlemen-like. I glance over at Erin who wipes her eyes with her sleeve. Instead of complying I bolt to the stairs, and I crash to the ground on the landing. Erin's laughter makes me smile with all my teeth.

Yay! I made her happy. This is fun.

Andre catches up to me. I giggle up at him, swinging my legs in the air. "See? My feet don't work anymore."

He shakes his head before helping me back to my useless feet. I stagger up the rest of the stairs and sprint down the wrong hallway.

"Please stop yelling. You're going to get yourself in trouble."

"Fight me." I pretend to box him, missing my punches and giggling more.

Andre grabs my hand, pulling me to my room. He stops in front of my door and looks in my eyes. "You ever need a ride, order a cab or call me. No one needs to be driving home after the bars." His serious tone almost sobers me up, their meaning finding the part of my brain that's sane.

Yet as quickly as the intensity rises, it dissipates. I grab my key from the clutch, but Andre takes it. He unlocks the door, cracks it open, and hands the key back to me.

"Thanks, Andre. You're a fine, Christian man—" I begin.

"Goodnight, Melanie. Be careful. Don't fall off your bed again."

Erin must have mentioned me falling from bed after a Taco Tuesday. Those darn tequila shots. They're brutal.

I stumble into my room, leaving Andre to close the door. No use changing my clothes–finding and putting on my pajamas is mission impossible–so I flop into bed with my borrowed clothes and giddy thoughts. *Look at me now, Brady. Going out to bars and not completely ruining stuff. Didn't think I could do it, huh? I showed you. But now you're the one missing out.*

Sleep overcomes my body before thoughts of Brady's brutal breakup with me can ruin my blissful, drunken night.

Chapter 9

October

The alarm is unmerciful at 7 a.m. My brain pounds against my skull, announcing another hangover. *What day is it? Ah, yes. Wednesday.* Taco Tuesdays always leave me in this sorry state. Hard liquor doesn't like me back.

I start my morning ritual of checking social media. With the screen brightness turned down, my phone tells me the news I dreaded but knew would happen eventually. The mattress drops out from under me or at least it feels like it. I don't cry; not yet at least.

I sprint to class without processing anything around me. Crossing the threshold of math class, I immediately approach Kat.

"Brady is in a relationship," I blurt out as I sit backward in the seat in front of her.

Kat swears. "Nooo. Who?"

"The one he told me not to worry about."

"That shi—"

Dylan strolls into the room, interrupting us. "Hey, Kat. Mel—"

"Not. Now. Dylan. Girl talk." Kat huffs as she waves him away. He rolls his eyes but sinks into a desk behind Kat. Kat sighs as she turns back to me. "Let's go shopping later. You need retail therapy. That will fix any broken heart."

Dylan doesn't say anything, casually straightening in his seat as the professor runs in oozing apologies; this signals the beginning of the next mind-numbing fifty minutes. I face the front and pretend to take notes during the lecture. I doodle in the corner of my notebook, anything to distract myself from Brady.

On the way to the mall later that day, music from the car's stereo blocks out my thoughts as Kat smokes a cigarette. A smokey car is the last thing I want, but causing any rifts in our friendship scares me. I can't lose her too. So, I let her do whatever she wants.

Kat speaks after a few minutes of silence. "So, was Brady your first heartbreak?" She lowers the speaker's volume and lets out a long puff of smoke.

"Yeah. I've only had one boyfriend," I admit, trying to focus on the road and not the tears forming in my eyes.

Kat wrinkles her nose. "Bleh. Men. Well, maybe that's what happened. He was sleeping with this chick from college when he couldn't be with you, and then he ended it with you. Guys do it all the time."

I gasp, and my stomach suddenly aches. *Was Brady cheating?*

"So, he had someone on the side the whole time. You were suspicious of her and now they are getting it in," Kat concludes, shrugging as if her allegation is no big deal.

Wincing at her words, I don't answer, and she falls quiet, hopefully catching the hint that this conversation is over. She doesn't bring it up even when we arrive at the mall and commence the shopping spree.

Kat takes the lead and walks straight into a store I've always passed by with its glaring, recessed ceiling lights, shiny tile, and stark white walls. Prim and proper. Nothing like the thrifted clothes on my body. Rubbing my sweaty hands on my secondhand jeans, I look around and find Kat browsing a clothes' rack. I join her, and the first item I grab is a basic gray T-shirt. The tag says "$34.99". Dang.

Definitely not my kind of store.

Kat holds up a black body suit to her. "You live in Montgomery Hall, right?" she asks as she examines the body suit and drapes it over her arm along with other clothes she already picked out. She grabs another body suit in a smaller size and shoves it at me.

I take it and say, "Yeah! I got sick the first week of school and the staff was so helpful."

"So, you know Nikki then?"

I choose my words carefully, unsure where Kat is going with this. "Not personally, but some of the dorm residents have said nice things."

Kat rolls her eyes. "They don't know what they're

talking about. Stay out of her way, especially if you come back to the dorm drunk. She'll write you up so fast, girl."

Oh, Kat is looking out for me. That's nice of her.

I grab a blush-color cropped sweater that I'm barely interested in, but I should have some clothes to try on like Kat.

I ask, "Do you know her?"

Kat leans over a merchandise table, so I can't see her face. "We used to hang out. Then she found Jesus and became holier than thou. Told me she didn't want to go out to the bars or drink and smoke anymore."

"That sucks." What else can I say? People change sometimes and leave us in the rubble of that friendship.

It's one of the deepest hurts I've ever felt.

"She runs her dorm like it's a church, expecting people to be good and follow her rules. Be on your best behavior if you cross paths with her."

I'd never been uncomfortable living at Montgomery Hall, but perhaps things are happening behind the scenes.

Kat stalks toward the dressing rooms without another word, her arms full of clothes. I snatch another body suit and a silky blouse then head to the dressing room myself. Every item I grabbed is mature and bar appropriate. So, not me.

"You better try on that bodysuit I handed you. You'll get everyone's attention in that," Kat comments from the changing room beside me.

I follow her advice, slipping on the black body suit and staring at myself in the mirror before trying on the next item. The clothing clings to every curve and line of my body leaving nothing to the imagination. I notice every piece of fabric that suctions to me. This is how people dress when they go out to the bars and clubs, and I need to be like them; not the academic girl who thrifts and goes to renaissance faires clad in medieval gowns.

I'll show Brady I can act like everyone else.

Kat exits the dressing room with the body suit in her hands, leaving the other clothes behind for a worker to put away. I hang up the clothes that didn't fit on the clothes' rack in the fitting room, but I purchase everything else.

RIP to my bank account.

Kat continues to another store, one full of makeup. I try to keep up with her fast pace, our shopping bags clutched in my hands. Talking and laughing about the mutual people we know passes the time while she drags me from store to store. A cloud of doubt dampens my spirits, but I hide behind my fake grin.

Kat stops to get a coffee, so naturally my mind wanders away from the present. Did Brady cheat? He often defended the person he's now dating. My mind races through the times he hung out with her like a movie montage of a detective gathering evidence: pictures on social media of them together and all the moments he casually mentioned being with her in our text conversations. I cringe. They probably weren't studying.

The most convicting proof—the formal I couldn't attend. A frat brother messaged me on social media, telling me Brady had showed up to the dance with her. I never confronted Brady about it. I ignored a lot of red flags. All because he said he cared and paid attention to lil ol' me.

What about me wasn't good enough, Brady?

We shop until I spend over a hundred dollars; my wardrobe needed major upgrading to keep up with the other girls. Our plastic bags practically drag along the ground of the mall's parking lot. Kat is unfazed by the bags resting up and down her arms.

"Yo, Kat!" someone calls as we approach my car. I see Isaac walking toward us.

Kat stands up on her tiptoes, ruffling his golden hair. "How's my favorite athlete?" she asks.

He flattens his hair and tries not to grin but fails. "Just saying hi. Need to buy some stuff from the sporting goods store." He stretches his arms into the air. "Oh, the team is having our first party of the year tomorrow night. You coming?"

"Wow, took you long enough to plan that. But I'll grace you with my presence." She turns to me as if she suddenly remembers I'm next to her. She adds, "Only if Melanie can come too."

He nods at me in recognition. "Oh, hey! You're from Spanish class. Yeah, sure. Should have enough space for one more person. Dylan's pre-gaming with us though."

Kat punches his shoulder. "Ah, you can have him."

"See you tomorrow. You know what time."

We part ways, and my now smoke-ridden car takes us back to Kat's place as she chatters about this and that.

She grabs her shopping bags from the back seat. "We can walk over to the party tomorrow," she says as she disappears into her condo. She never mentioned plans for tonight, but I need a distraction, one of alcoholic proportions.

I drive back to the dorm and text Dani to see if she wants to go out tonight. I lay on my bed for a while before I hear back from her.

Dani: "I have a meet tomorrow. I'm sorry."

This is a typical reply from her. Swimming and hanging out with her fellow swimmers keep her occupied.

That's fine. I'll text Hayley and Alex. It's been a while since I've talked to them.

Me: "Guys, you won't believe what happened."

Instead of questions, they send me a picture of them from this year's Renaissance faire. Grins light up their faces as they pose in front of a massive black throne shaped as if it were made of swords.

Hayley: "Wish you could have been here last week. The turkey legs weren't the same without you."

Alex: "It was so fun this year."

They never ask what happened. My heart sinks. No

affirmation or alcohol to deter me from floundering in gloominess tonight.

My stomach growls while I finish math homework. Ignoring my hunger and my thoughts of Brady, I watch a romcom. It mostly works until bedtime when I have nothing left to distract me. The tears arrive as I lay down, snot and regret my company for the night instead of someone I love.

Dreams find me as the night blurs into disfigured memories holding me down to relive what I'll never see or experience again. Brady smiles at me and pulls me into his warm embrace.

But not in reality. His arms hold someone else now.

Chapter 10

First Lacrosse House Party

Kat meets me at the dorm late Thursday evening, the sun long gone as we walk to the lacrosse team's party. Between liquor shots from mini bottles that she discards on the ground and puffs of cigarette smoke, Kat explains that the team stays in a school-purchased apartment complex across campus.

My newly acquired heels wobble on the concrete sidewalk; always one misstep away from a broken ankle. I concentrate on my footsteps as goosebumps spread over my arms and legs; this sleeveless dress isn't the wisest clothing choice for a Midwest October night. Kat is undaunted by the weather and her own heels, marching a few steps ahead.

I wish I had her confidence.

Campus ends revealing several blocks of homes before we stand at their apartment building where light and music pour from its windows. Kat grabs my hand, pulling me through the open door into the lobby. Well, it was a lobby before, but it has been renovated into a hang out area. A Billiards and ping pong table, a sitting area with a tv, chairs, cheap couches, and a long table fill the remodeled lobby. Some people linger here, but the party lies beyond through another door to an expansive outdoor space.

My jaw drops. In one corner, people play sand volleyball, and the other side has several tables set up for beer pong. Lawn chairs, picnic tables, a barbecue pit, bubbling hot tub, and an outdoor, covered mini bar occupy the rest of the area. No wonder the lacrosse team throws good parties. They have the best space for it, even compared to the fraternities' mansions, as if this was built specifically for a good time. It would be perfect in warmer weather, but thankfully space heaters and a fire pit warm the area; the body count also helps.

The university treats their athletes a little too well.

Kat snorts beside me. "Close your mouth. You might drool."

She probably doesn't see my eyes roll as she pushes her way through the crowd to the mini bar; I am her shadow as always. My body buzzes from the one shot I took on an empty stomach before we got here. Kat shoves another shot bottle into my hand, grabs one for herself, and we immediately drink them. The liquor burns, but I rarely turn down anything offered to me if I know where it comes from.

"Hey, Kat!" someone shouts from the nearest beer pong table. Isaac waves us over where Dylan and the other teammate from my Spanish class are setting up a game. I can't remember his name. Must be the alcohol already clouding my mind.

Kat beams, placing her arm around Isaac's shoulder, or at least trying because he towers over her. "Told you I would be here," she says.

"Yeah, yeah. Why don't you play beer pong with us? Someone needs to be on Dylan's team."

Kat's eyes light up. "Actually, I'm looking for someone. But Melanie here is a world class beer pong player. She'll carry Dylan to certain victory."

I cover my face with my hands as the guys look at me with certain skepticism.

"Bye, bye!" Kat disappears into the smoke and music. She's always searching for ways to set me up with her brother.

I fold my arms around myself, avoiding eye contact. "Okay. She obviously lied. I'm a newbie," I confess.

Isaac laughs. "Well, if that's the case we will put you with Dylan so he can lose for once."

I glance at Dylan who smirks but says nothing as he finishes arranging the cups.

The other teammate reaches his hand out to me. "I'm Ben by the way. You help us with Spanish homework, but I've never formally introduced myself outside of class."

"I'm Melanie. Oh. You already know that. Uh, nice to officially meet you," I stammer, shaking his hand. He grins, his teeth perfectly straight, his smile inviting and warm. Something about guys always makes me so tongue-tied. How embarrassing.

"Okay, I'll explain the rules to the noob," Dylan says breaking me from my prolonged eye contact with Ben.

Dylan tells me how to play, but I'm only half-listening. The music, laughter, and liquor don't make focusing easy.

"You ready?" Dylan asks, and I nod, probably looking like a deer in headlights as I stand next to him while across the table Isaac and Ben have their ping pong balls ready in hand.

"Bouncing or not?" Ben asks.

Dylan shrugs. "Both is fine this round."

Ben tosses it, and it bounces off the cup's rim. Isaac's ball does the same. I grab them from the ground nearby, handing one to Dylan.

"Ladies first," he says, watching me.

I stand with my feet apart, my heart pounding because, of course, I would take a beer pong game too seriously. I gulp and throw the ball across the table, and it lands neatly in one of the cups closest to me. I cheer but instantly cover my mouth. Ben whistles while Isaac grabs the cup and drinks it. Dylan smiles at me, his dimples prominent even in the low light.

"I'll be darned. Beginner's luck." He throws his ball, and it brushes the side of a cup.

"It's like you're the main character or something," Isaac jokes as he retrieves the balls.

I mock bow. "Thank you, thank you. That will probably not happen again."

My prediction is right. The game continues, getting worse the more cups of beer that we drink. It's unsanitary, but I don't think about it once. Dylan scores the most points while I don't land any more of my shots. Ben and Isaac lose the game regardless. Are they not trying on purpose to make me feel better? I hold my hand up and Dylan returns the high-five.

Isaac sets up the game for another round. "Okay, I want Dylan this time. My self-esteem needs a boost after that."

Dylan and Ben switch places. And–no surprise–Isaac and Dylan win even though I make two shots this game.

I laugh as I chug the last beer cup. I point at Dylan. "When did you get so good at beer pong?"

Dylan shrugs, looking away from me without an answer. I don't have time to wonder about it as Isaac runs over to the mini bar and grabs three shots. He hands them to Ben and me. "To Dylan and his beer pong supremacy."

Isaac cheers, and we take the shots as Dylan shifts back and forth on his feet with his hands in his pockets.

"Alright. I'm going inside for Billiards," Dylan

announces.

Ben turns to me. "Want to join us?"

My body feels like it's rocking as I turn to survey the area. A group of strangers stand by the volleyball court. My brain forms a terrible idea.

I wave them away. "I'm joining the volleyball game actually."

Dylan clears his throat. "Sure about that? You're literally swaying."

In answer, I stumble to the sand pit, my heels puncturing the grass below me. I ask the group of strangers, "Are we playing or standing around?" I slip my heels off and throw them to the ground.

I'm rewarded with a few chuckles, and everyone splits into teams. I join the one with the least amount of people.

Dylan is right. This is a bad idea.

Every time I serve, the ball refuses to go over the net, and anytime I stand in front, it soars above me no matter how high I jump. At the end of the second game, the volleyball flies at me. Instead of getting out of the way or hitting it, I use my shoulder to block it. It rams into my shoulder, and I fall into the sand. Chuckles echo in my head, and the world swirls around me.

Too much alcohol and athletics for me.

One of the guys on my team helps me to my feet. I try to steady myself in the shifting sand, but my body rocks back and forth.

"No offense, but you should sit this one out. Get yourself some water too," the guy suggests as he guides me off the court and rejoins the game.

I snatch my heels from the ground. Pain radiates in my shoulder as the party whirls around me: flashing lights, music more base than anything else, and pieces of conversations I can't piece together. Where can a girl get some peace and quiet around here?

Staggering through the quad–everyone is calling it that–I reach for the door, but it opens and the person coming outside bumps into me, spilling their drink on my torso. They don't apologize and keep walking.

What a day to wear a white dress.

The darkness outside will cover me, but the noise is overwhelming. I reenter the apartment, liquid clinging to my skin as I shiver. *Where's Kat and a place to sober up?* The hang out area bursts with people, so I trip up the stairs toward the bedrooms. The hallway gives the stillness I've searched for. Without hesitation I lean against the wall and slide down, sitting alone in the lacrosse team's apartment complex with a drink-stained dress and a headache.

I text Kat asking her whereabouts, but she doesn't respond. Minutes pass when I hear someone coming my way. Peeking my eyes open, I observe Dylan ushering someone into a room; whoever they are, I only catch a glimpse of a long brunette ponytail.

Dylan notices me. "Oh, wow. Someone had a rough night."

I throw my hands in the air, my shoulder complaining from the movement. "Beginner's luck only applies to beer pong, not actual sports."

He walks over, eyeing my ruined outfit. He extends his hand, and I stand with his help. Wobbling, I grab the wall next to me.

"Stay here and I'll get you something clean," Dylan says as he disappears into his bedroom. I don't listen to him though. When the door shuts, I sneak closer. A female voice is speaking behind the closed door.

I wonder who that is. What if it's that woman Harrison is so infatuated with? What's her name? Lauren? He mentioned she was messing around with a lacrosse player. For some reason, my stomach drops at the thought. The idea of Dylan with someone else makes me...

The door opens, and I startle. Dylan hands me a T-shirt and athletic shorts as he stands in front of the door, blocking whoever is in the room with him.

"Hopefully the shorts fit. There's a public bathroom down the hall," he explains.

"Thanks," I mumble as I take the clothes from him.

"Goodnight." He shuts the door, and the female says something to him, high-pitched and angry. He responds, his tone sounding more annoyed than anything else. I shuffle to the bathroom, ready to get out of this sticky dress.

Kat never texts me back.

I'm only minutes from campus. I don't need to waste money on a cab, I rationalize as I change into Dylan's clothes. *I can walk a few blocks by myself. I'm an adult. I don't need someone to hold my hand through everything.*

Donning my new-to-me shirt and athletic shorts smelling like laundry detergent and faint hints of cologne, I walk into the cold night, heels in my hand; I probably look hilarious to any onlooker. The party rages behind me, showing no signs of stopping soon. The further I walk away, the quieter the night becomes. The streetlamps provide minimal light and plenty of shadows. I swallow the acid rising in my throat from the alcohol and festering fear.

This isn't a good idea.

Did I make a wrong turn? My intoxicated mind plays tricks on me, every shadow shifting and creeping. As if an answer to my panic, I hear car tires behind me; my peripheral vision confirms it's a large vehicle. These little legs can only move so fast. My heartbeat thumps in my ears along to the car's slow, deliberate movement. They should have passed me.

Well, it was nice being alive while it lasted.

A truck pulls up beside me, and someone says, "Melanie," as they roll down the window.

I see the driver and set a hand on my chest as I find my breath. "Andre. You scared me."

"Sorry about that. I wasn't sure how to do that without freaking you out," he says. "Why are you walking out here?"

"I am returning from a party. How did you know it was me?" I ask.

He grins. "Who else would rather take off their heels and get their feet dirty than try to walk with those shoes across campus? Or it was the height."

I roll my eyes, and he laughs. He asks, "Do you need a ride to the dorm? You're a little... off course. Landed in a neighborhood next to campus."

So much for being an independent adult who doesn't need anyone.

I wave him away. "It's okay. If you could point me in the right direction I can..."

"You're shoeless, don't have any mace, and lost. Please think again."

I throw my hands up in defeat, walking to the passenger side. Andre hops out of the truck and appears at my side, opening the door and helping me up the step and into the truck. Country music plays from the speakers. I chuckle while Andre puts the car into drive.

"What's so funny?" he asks as he pulls away from the neighborhood and back to campus.

"I never pictured you as a country music fan."

"Wait. Let me fix that for you." He grabs his phone and taps on it, the song changing into a full-blown gospel choir hit. "This better?"

"You said it, not me." A fresh wave of nausea hits me. I better not throw up in his truck. To distract myself I ask, "What're you doing out so late?"

"Couldn't sleep. Sometimes taking a drive on the backroads around town and some prayer helps." He hums along to the song. "But really. I meant it. If you ever need a ride home, even if it's across campus, I would rather you call me. Or take a cab at least."

A blush flares on my cheeks, shame settling into its familiar throne in the pit of my stomach and chest. He's right. I shouldn't have walked home alone, inebriated, and unprepared to deal with unwanted attention.

He sighs. "I don't mean to sound like a strict parent. I care about your safety…which sounds exactly like a strict parent."

"That's it?"

He briefly studies me before returning his attention to the road. "I'm not sure what you're getting at. You can make your own choices. But sometimes, alcohol makes those choices unsafe for you and others around you."

I lean my achy head against the cool window. "Must be great not to have any vices."

Andre snorts. "We all have our vices. I'm just trying to deny mine."

He switches the music back to country, the soft acoustic guitar and twangy voice lulling me into a quiet stupor on our way back to the dorm. Andre helps me out of the truck and walks me to my room.

My thoughts linger on Andre as I collapse into bed, forgoing changing into my pajamas and brushing my teeth. I want the warmth and safety of my bed. And Dylan's shirt smells, well, nice.

So, Andre is trying to deny his vices, huh? What a different view than many of the people I've met here. My peers run after every high, any indulgence without hesitation. What is moderation? But I can't judge them. I've been following in their footsteps, wanting to be included, wanting the friendship and romance that lies beyond the bottom of an empty bottle and a vacant bed. What gives Andre the willpower to say no?

A text message lights up my phone.

Dylan: "Did you make it back okay?"

I fall asleep before I can reply.

Chapter 11

Unfortunately, I don't have Andre's willpower to say no. The next day I'm trailing Kat into a cocktail bar that the fraternities frequent according to her. She wants to take someone home tonight—her words, not my assumptions. Unlike the clubs that frazzle my senses, this bar possesses a classy vibe: exposed brick and antique wood paneling throughout, checkered tile, leather bar stools and velvet couches, a cherry wood counter stretching from the entrance to the back, and jazz music welcoming my ears.

I've stepped into the 1920s. *How delightful. Where's my pearl necklace and cloche hat? I'm sure Gatsby is around somewhere.*

Kat pulls me away from my reverie to the bar, ordering two cocktails. "I'm surprised they didn't question your ID. This place is a little stricter with minors. Guess they need money."

I glance around us, hoping the staff didn't hear her. Gripping the counter, I sigh and try to let go of any pent-up feelings. Kat never apologized for ditching me last at

115

the lacrosse party nor did she mention anything about it. Granted, I could have called a cab or someone to pick me up. My pride–and wallet–wouldn't allow common sense.

What's the point of being angry at her? It won't change anything, and I don't want to drive any kind of wedge between us. Besides, I won't be thinking about it once I have some liquor in my stomach.

Kat bumps her shoulder against mine. "Hey, cheer up. We're in fraternity territory. I need you on your best behavior. Can't have gloomy company ruining the night."

The bartender slides the drinks to us, deflating any tension in me. She's right. I've yet to be invited to a fraternity party, my name on the weekly coveted guest list. Kat throws back her cocktail like it's a shot, while I savor the fruity flavor. She orders a shot while I lean against the bar, surveying the room.

Despite the cigarette smoke wafting throughout the establishment, I recognize some peers near one of the larger booths. Kat takes the shot, and I signal her, pointing at Harrison and Seth who sit among people who I assume are their frat brothers. She grabs my hand, my heels almost not finding the ground as she drags me over to them. Harrison and Seth stand when they see us, Kat scooting into the booth without hesitation. She strikes up a conversation with the guy next to her.

I remain standing, wanting to showcase my height from the heels. "I'm on your turf tonight," I say to them.

To my right, Harrison gestures with a beer bottle. "This place is one of my favorites. Can actually have a conversation here."

Seth shrugs from my left, taking a sip of his beer. "It's too quiet."

"You'll have your fill of noise at the party tomorrow." Harrison laughs at him. I set down my empty cocktail glass, and Harrison grabs a bottle from the ice bucket full of beers on the table. He pulls a bottle opener from his pant pocket and flicks the lid off. I watch the lid fall to the ground as he hands me the beer. He makes no move to pick it up, so I let it be.

Harrison blurts out some Greek Letters I can't remember then says, "…is having a party. Costumes too. You in?"

My pulse quickens, and I glance over at Kat, still idly chatting. She doesn't realize I'm about to make her week. I have secured the prized invitation to a fraternity party. Finally!

A grin dominates my face, but I can't help it. "Kat and I would love to go. Thanks for the invite." I begin to take a sip of my drink.

"Nothing like someone's first frat party," Seth exclaims, extending his hand. His beer bottle shoots forward, knocking into mine. Pain radiates from my mouth, specifically my front teeth from the glasses colliding.

Before I can say something or react, Harrison pats my shoulder, the one I hurt last night in volleyball. I wince as he says, "I'll get you on the list for tomorrow. Should be able to squeeze you both in."

I thank him again and excuse myself to the bathroom, examining my mouth in the dim light.

Yep, I'm staring at a chip in my right front tooth.

I leave the bathroom wondering what to do about my dental dilemma to find Kat standing at the entrance, hands on her hips. "It's too quiet. Let's find someplace a little livelier," she says, flinging open the door and walking across the street to the blaring of car horns.

I wave at the guys and reluctantly follow, my heart pounding as we make it to the other side of the street without incident.

When we're safe on the sidewalk, I announce, "Did you hear? I got us into a frat party. You have to dress in a costume too."

Kat pumps her first in the air. "Whoo hoo. I've been to plenty of frat parties." She must see the annoyance on my face because she adds, "But it's been a while."

My excitement deflates as we hand the sport bar's bouncer our IDs. So much for doing something nice for her. I don't have much time to think about it as Kat heads straight to the bar and orders for us. We drink until the world swirls around me, and I don't think about the fraternity party or Kat's behavior anymore.

The night rages on. Kat finds some of her friends at the same bar eventually. I don't know any of them personally, barely recognizing faces as the liquor blurs my cognition. Someone's hand brushes my butt, resting it there for a moment. One of Kat's companions makes a comment about my behind, and I laugh along. Always laughing, always cheerful. Drunk Melanie is a crowd pleaser.

Alcohol makes small violations not so disrespectful. It becomes a joke or a mistake. Only an unwanted hand on your butt for a little too long, and all I can do is laugh.

And forget where I am.

~ ~ ~

Homework consumes my Saturday until I drive to Kat's apartment. When she opens the door, a blush creeps on my face. She's dressed up in a costume, unlike me. I even ditched my heels tonight in favor of my high-top sneakers. My achy feet have had enough of wearing heels for one week.

"Sorry. I don't have a proper costume for a frat party," I confess to the hula-girl before me.

Kat waves me inside the apartment, her short leaf-printed skirt swooshing with the motion. I follow her to her room, and she plops onto the vanity seat. "Chill out. Okay. So, you're wearing black. And I have cat ears. You can be—"

I stand next to her and stare into the mirror. "Unsexy

Cat," I reply without hesitation.

Kat puts a hand on my shoulder, the most comforting gesture she has ever shown me. "Don't be so down on yourself. You don't need a man to feel sexy."

At least she's being kind about my insecurities and not changing the subject to her this time.

I shrug. "It's original. I don't want to be sexy anyway." I don't know if my lie is convincing enough, but I also don't care if she believes me. I'm exhausted from competing with the other girls who are more stunning and charming, more everything than me. I try so hard and for them, it's effortless.

I rub my finger along my smudged eyeliner and decide not to share my feelings with her. Kat stands and ducks into the closet for a moment, pulling out the cat ears and waving them at me. I take them but don't put them on. She doesn't pry further into my insecurities which I'm grateful for. I've said enough.

Kat grabs a shot bottle from the kitchen, unscrews it, and gulps it down. She burps. "Well, forget Brady. It's our night. Let's get some smoothies."

That's random because we're about to go to a party, but I accept the distraction from my negative thoughts. I sit in her car's passenger seat, the cat ears clasped in my hands. As we park at the smoothie restaurant and walk in, her comment makes sense; we are getting alcoholic smoothies.

The Ugly Smoothie—known for its healthy, no additive smoothies by day, and its alcoholic smoothies by night according to its marketing plastered over the restaurant and menus. *What a strategic business in a college town. Breakfast and booze. Yes, please!*

Kat shoos me out; a sign warns us they will ask for an ID from anyone in the store getting a drink at this hour and, somehow, I forgot my ID at the dorm. *She downed a shot before coming here. Was it her first of the night,* I wonder as I return to the passenger seat. Kat hops into the car not much later, holding a smoothie cup for each of us. She hands me mine: a strawberry banana rum concoction.

"Drink it fast. It's already melting," she insists as she weaves around town toward the block where the fraternity houses beckon like a spotlight.

I barely taste the smoothie as I place it in the drink holder. Brady's new relationship and dubbing myself as Unsexy Cat sabotages any good experience that alcohol can give me. I place the cat ears on my head and stare out the window. I pull one leg onto the seat, wrapping my arms around it. Distraction. That's what I need tonight. Anything to take my mind off the guy who lied and didn't stay.

Fraternity parties are a new environment to me, a whole different beast from Kat's condo and bars. I want to keep my wits about me. *I'll leave the drink in here. Don't want to be unaware in a strangers' mansion with hundreds of people and those with wandering hands.*

The frat houses come into view, dominating the whole city block. Kat curses multiple times as she searches for a place to park. After a few failed attempts, she stops the car in front of a fire hydrant, parks, and we follow the sounds of people talking over each other.

A crowd oozes along the sidewalk and the street, taking up every inch of space. Who thought it was a good idea to build fraternity houses right next to each other? *This body count is a hazard*, I think as I dodge a group of guys sprinting along the sidewalk.

I have never seen so many nurses and cat ears in my life, either. *Unsexy Cat is more original,* I assure myself. We stand in front of Harrison's house, the line shrinking as people disperse; the rejects either running off to find acceptance into another party or stand to the side of the house hoping to find another way in.

Kat pushes to the front door, butting in front of a few people. "Kat and Melanie," she says with hands on her hips.

The bouncer–a frat brother–glances down at his list and shakes his head in dismissal. Kat gives him the finger as we join a herd of castoffs swelling against the house, ready to push down its walls to join the party.

Rejected. Of course.

I guess Harrison forgot. No surprise though—this feeling is familiar. The high school parties didn't exactly require my attendance. I spent my time writing for the school paper and yearbook. Honor student. The theater kids' loyal stagehand. I wasn't nobody, but I wasn't somebody either. I existed, and the cycle continues.

The crowd of bystanders grows until we are shoved onto the porch, wondering about our next move. Suddenly, a side door opens to reveal a familiar face. We scramble inside and the door closes before the flood can enter. Only a few bodies make it through to the coveted party.

I'd recognize that smirk anywhere. Dylan to the rescue.

He acknowledges Kat and I with a brief tip of his hat before vanishing into the swarm of humans. I follow Kat into the frenzy that is the infamous frat party. Potent perfume and marijuana fill the space not occupied by a person. Lights are uncommon in this mansion coddling overworked, intoxicated young adults. Kat pulls me onto the enticing dance floor: a room bursting with long tables that people dance on top of with its strobing fluorescent lights matching my heartbeat. The music presses against us. I can't concentrate on anything around me, my brain overstimulated by every sound, sight, touch, and smell emanating from this one room.

Two guys appear beside us. Their voices compete with the music, and Kat takes their flirty bait by grabbing the guy nearest to her. She throws her emptied smoothie under the tables pushed together to create a platform of sorts then drags him up on the tables with her.

"I'm...What is..." the guy left behind with me says while his eyes wander up and down my body. He leans inches away from me.

Not today. Unsexy Cat wants her freedom.

I stand on my tiptoes and hoist my legs up onto the table; my last glimpse of the floor is him rolling his eyes. I swirl around and around while strangers press against me on every side a few feet above the ground. Not alone but lonely in a room bursting from young adults trying to feel something. There's nothing but the pressure of bodies and the music.

Kat appears among the flashing lights. She drags me off the table and away with the guy she's claiming for the night. He leads us past the double doors to a hallway of bedrooms like we are VIPs. A guy slumped on the couch occupies the room we enter. His glassy eyes fixate on a blank television screen.

Kat's man laughs. "This is my roommate Philip. Oh, it's his birthday."

Excited to see a familiar face, I exclaim, "Happy Birthday Philip!"

He doesn't acknowledge me or anyone else.

Kat gulps down a drink she's given, but I politely refuse several times.

"Come ooon. I need to smoke," Kat whines as she

pulls the guy from the room, making her way to the nearest balcony with me right behind. Philip doesn't move or utter a noise. He's on something a little more potent than alcohol alone surely.

On the balcony, clouds of smoke sting my eyes as I stand above the party and soberly observe. A quote arises in my mind: "A multitude of people and yet a solitude." I understand now what Dickens tried to convey.

This is what it's like to be sober among drunks. There's the deliberate overstimulation of every sense leading me to hypervigilance; I'm probably the only one not plastered in this house. Lonely in a mansion full of people, surveying the big picture and details they will grasp to remember and piece together in the morning. The laughs—the ones that start in the mouth and end in the belly. The mistakes—touching, kissing, and all that leads to. I am the sole witness to it.

I wish I didn't know some of the things that happen.

As the night drags out, the party surges; somehow more people fit into this bursting mansion. Kat has long ditched me, so I wander around searching for anyone I know. At some point Harrison stands ahead of me, but he's surrounded by a group of people. Their obvious drunken laughter and poise intimidate me, nervousness keeping me from joining them. I roll my eyes at my own cowardice while I seek out one of those game rooms to occupy myself with until Kat drives us home or I order a cab.

Why am I here?

"Hey, Melanie!" a familiar voice calls to me.

I peek into a room as Dylan leans over a pool table, assembling the balls for a solo game. A single beer rests on top of a mini fridge in the corner of the room. He's wearing gym shorts–shocker–and a red, white, and blue hat with a single star on it.

I join him by the table, picking up one of the pool balls from the plastic triangle. "Where's your crew?" I ask.

He shrugs, grabbing his pool stick. "Around, hopefully. I'm playing one last game before rounding up whoever is left to take them home."

"Proud of you. You're a proper mother hen."

He rolls his eyes. "Wow. Thanks for that character assessment. I could be super judgmental of your so-called costume, but I'll be kind."

"I'm Unsexy Cat. It's original. Who are you—"

"Where's Kat?"

"Somewhere in this fire-hazard." I sigh, gesturing to the house and letting him change the subject. "Not sure when she'll be ready to go. My phone died too." I replace the ball and grab the other pool stick. "While I wait for her, can you teach me how to play?"

He grabs a drink from the mini fridge. "Sure but drink a beer first. You could win sober." He hands me the beer and adds, "I can take you home if she doesn't stumble in here soon."

Andre's warning about drunk driving echoes in my mind. Kat, her friends, and I have broken that rule several times since then, but being sober makes it more real, like bad things will happen to anyone at any time. Is this safe?

Noticing my silence, Dylan holds his hands up.

"Don't worry. I'm not drunk. This is my second beer. And over a few hours, that's nothing," he quietly assures me.

I nod and wipe my sweaty hands on my leggings. He wouldn't lie to me, right?

Dylan lifts the triangle. "Okay then. Balls are racked. Let's get down to business, shall we? So, when playing pool…"

He thoroughly explains the rules but as the game commences and we sip the beers, it only gets worse the longer we play; it's not the liquor but our own goofiness that turns the game from serious to a joke. Trick shots take over any normal competition. At some point, I sit in the middle of the table as the balls roll past me and into the pockets; that's what the holes in the table are called according to Dylan. The best part is I've had a few sips of an alcoholic smoothie and one beer, but I am completely in control and aware.

His back rests against mine now. We remain like that, back-to-back, talking about nothing important, while the party goes on without us. Dylan and I are surrounded by people but somehow in solitude. This moment is more real than the liquor-saturated, gossip-tainted nights I've found myself participating in more and more. Tonight, there's no unwanted touching or advances, questioning if I'm safe, or ambiguity and wondering what happened the night before.

Just Dylan and I and this moment.

Dylan's laugh shakes my body, bringing me back to the present moment. "Well, Kat texted me back saying she left the building with someone. I'll take you back to the dorm unless you prefer a cab. You can use my phone—"

"It's only midnight, surely! The night is young, *mi amigo*." I joke as a yawn escapes my mouth.

His feet hit the floor. "Well, let's round up any teammates left. And you can come back to my place if you want." He grabs my pool stick and places it next to his on the table, replaces the balls into the triangle rack, then throws away our empty beer bottles.

Did he really invite me back to his apartment? Even though he had someone over the other night. Then it occurs to me—this is the first time Dylan and I would be alone-alone. He's impossible to read. Unsexy Cat shouldn't keep her hopes up for anything. *What am I expecting from this anyway,* I wonder as he gestures for me to follow him in search of his teammates.

He's inviting me over, and I don't want to say no. Heat rushes to my face as I nod and leave the game room with him. We find several of his friends scattered around the mansion participating in various activities. Dylan and I drag the begrudging teammates into Isaac's car–he informs me several times that the SUV is his–and Dylan drives us to the team's apartment. Dylan turns on some punk rock music, and the car vibrates with the guys' drunken wailing. I laugh at their failed attempts to remember the lyrics, thankful Dylan suggested I sit up front away from the rowdiness.

I watch Dylan, observing as he drives home with a concentrated expression on his face. *What is he thinking about? Why is he bringing me along?* I ruminate about the woman he had in his room a few nights ago at the party. I can ask him, but I can't find the right words. He turns his head to me at a stop light, and I bite my lip, looking away as soon as his eyes meet mine. I hum along to the song to distract myself.

Dylan parks the van, and we herd his friends into their respective rooms. As we walk to his room, the only sound is our footsteps and my increasing heartbeat, a stark comparison to the raging frat party minutes earlier.

He unlocks and opens the door. "Yeah. It's a mess. Sorry. Find somewhere to sit if you can. I'll be right back," he apologizes as he ducks into the bathroom.

I sit on the edge of Dylan's bed, picking at my nails and observing the room to distract my nerves. It's a typical single guy's room: the clothes and lacrosse gear covering a chair in the corner; a television paired with a gaming console; unusable desk cluttered with anything but schoolwork; a laundry basket erupting with clothes next to the closet instead of being hung up. One difference breaks the common athlete archetype, which is the comic books lining a bookshelf and a superhero movie poster hanging above his bed.

From the corner of my eye, I notice a picture frame on his bedside table. I lean closer to study it. Three children pose at the end of a dock. One girl and two boys who could be identical twins. *That must be Dylan and Kat as kids. But who is the third person? A cousin? I wonder…*

The bathroom door creaks open, and I jump back from the picture frame, adjusting myself back on the edge of his bed. Dylan walks back into the room, but his hat and shirt are missing, and he wears sweats. Holy abs too. I stare somewhere above his head. I'm sure I seem like a pubescent girl with the way I'm gawking. Abs are nothing new.

Calm down, Melanie. What a way to ruin this one and only chance with Dylan.

To distract myself I ask, "So…who is your favorite superhero?"

He stands in front of me, hands resting on his lean hips. "You noticed. Darn. My guilty pleasure."

Dylan grabs a comic from his bedside table with the picture frame on it. He points to a man in a tight red, white, and blue suit with several stars who holds a large, metallic shield. He shrugs, trying to downplay his interest.

"Patriotism. America. So lame."

"No. No, it's not." I quietly exhale, releasing the pressure in my chest before looking him in the eyes and wondering if he knows this evening with him has been one of the most authentic moments I've had in college. An athlete who likes comic books is letting me into his world. No liquor or other substances involved.

Dylan gazes down at me with an increasingly intense gaze, studying me. I want to tell him the thoughts swirling through my mind, but I'm losing focus.

Breath hitched in my chest, I sit straighter and whisper, "This is what you enjoy. How can that be lame?"

He leans closer, and my heart feels like it's knocking against my chest; that familiar knot ties itself in my stomach. His hands rest on either side of my legs. I'm acutely aware of the way he smells up close—sweet like a coffee shop, somehow. With his hat gone, his hair cascades into envy-inducing curls. My cat ears haven't left my head.

Then the thoughts begin. *Stop getting your hopes up. Say something else. He doesn't see you like that. Unsexy Cat doesn't get the guy. And he was clearly with someone the other night.*

But he's so close and if I stretch a little further then...

"Is this okay?" His lips hover over mine, but my insecurities fail me.

"What about that girl the other night?" I ask.

Good job, Melanie. You blew it.

He smiles, but it doesn't reach his eyes. "Oh. That was my ex. She wanted to argue about something in private then left."

"Oh." This is all I manage to say along with a nod of consent.

His lips find mine before we finish our conversation. We don't speak for a while. Unsexy Cat somehow got the guy tonight. What I keep to myself during those moments is that I think of one person, and it isn't the one I am with. Memories of Brady always resurface at the worst of times.

Because that's where Dylan and I lost each other—ending before truly beginning.

Chapter 12

The Morning After

Sunday morning welcomes me with weak sunshine and a chilly breeze as I walk across campus with cat ears clutched in my hand. My leggings were lost among the clothes on Dylan's floor, so I borrowed his gym shorts. Again. He didn't wake up when I left.

My thoughts are my only company on this walk; in the daylight the route from his apartment to campus is less confusing. Inevitably, my mind recalls last night. It was unexpected, but I like Dylan. My heart flutters in my chest at the confession. *I like Dylan.* Where did that come from? Somewhere between classes, some meals together, the parties, and nights out at the bars, I developed an attachment to Dylan; probably too quickly, but whoever said feelings are logical? Ruminating on Brady kept me from seeing what is right in front of me.

Because who wants to be let down like that a second time?

I shiver and wrap my arms tighter around myself,

deciding not to dwell further on Brady. Nothing good can come from that.

The dorm offers warmth from the cold, and as soon as I'm in my room, I grab my phone. I text Kat, explaining the situation. She doesn't reply after an hour, so I send a follow up message.

Me: "Should I text Dylan?"

Kat: "Nah."

Thanks for the support, I think as I unclench my fists, trying to settle the annoyance bubbling in me. She's my closest friend here. I shouldn't be mad at her, but she ditched me in an unfamiliar environment. Again. Sure, she's comfortable in those situations; that was my first time at a frat party. Do I talk to her about it? Will she think I'm childish if I tell her it "hurt my feelings" that she left me at a party?

Something about this pair of siblings makes me anxious. *Because I enjoy conflict and the steep possibility of rejection.* That's where I find myself these days, and I can't get out of this without facing it like an adult.

So, I do what I do best—ignore it.

Distractions are easy to find. I pace around my little room; check the scale and compare the number against the notes I keep on my weight; scroll through social media; text Alex and Hayley to tell them about my first frat party excluding details about Dylan; I even rearrange my bookshelf. Anything to avoid these budding emotions of affection, anger, and disappointment somehow coexisting.

Late Sunday afternoon rolls around before his name flashes across my phone's screen. I swipe open the message without hesitation.

Dylan: "Have a game today. A practice one with the team. Kat's going. You in?"

I reply with an "Okay" quicker than my brain can process what it's doing. As soon as the text *swooshes* to Dylan's phone, I'm ready to smack myself for replying that fast. *Way to be desperate.* I pace and wait for his answer.

He promptly replies within a few seconds. **Dylan:** "5 pm."

Nothing endearing or hinting at him truly wanting me at the game. *An invitation is enough*, I tell myself. I'm already expecting too much from someone who may or may not be interested. I sigh, the butterflies in my stomach settling. I'm not sure where we stand, relationally speaking. People sleep with other people all the time. It's more complicated for me. I've grown fond of Dylan and his stupid smirk and how his curls stick out from under his hat.

I can't shut off my feelings.

Wait. What should I wear to the game? Should I dress cute or for the weather? I don't want to give the impression that I'm trying to get his attention. Besides, he'll be focused on the game. Should I write his number on my face? That's what I used to do for Brady's baseball games.

Maybe he secretly thought it was childish, and Dylan might think the same thing.

Somehow, my indecision doesn't keep me from writing Dylan's jersey number on my face–I had seen it on his jersey in his room–because I'm being silly and a little brave. He could be interested too, right? We'd go on a few dates and have some fun.

Dumb little crush. Dumb little me.

Kat texts me around 4:30 p.m.: "Meet me outside your dorm."

Getting ready doesn't take long, so I sit on a bench outside the dorm and read. A cool breeze stirs the pages; I chose wisdom and wore warmer clothing. Loud chatter catches my attention minutes later. Glancing up, I spot Kat and her posse–people closer to her age that she hangs out with often–walking toward me. They pass by without acknowledging me, including Kat. I drop my book in my messenger bag before she can comment about me being a nerd for reading for fun. They converse amongst themselves while I trail them to the lacrosse field. Their faces I recognize, but their names escape me; this group tends to hang out with Kat without me. Small talk is pointless.

Now I feel stupid with this jersey number on my face.

We sit in the second row of bleachers framing the lacrosse field, and Kat speaks to me for the first time since walking there with each other.

"He's making me keep score. The only reason I'm here," she complains.

I just nod at her and turn my attention to the field.

A sparse crowd shows up for this scrimmage, the school's lacrosse team split in half to compete against each other; all for practice and love of the game. The teams take the field, and Kat's distant mood switches for the better as she cheers for Dylan. We yell and clap the whole game as if it's real; it keeps us warmer than sitting and spectating. Dylan and Isaac score most of the goals for their team. Kat tallies the points and confirms that Dylan's team wins after the hour-long game.

The crowd thins, and the players disperse from the field. Kat pulls me to the locker room, where she bursts through its door and yells, "Nice plays, boys!"

Her posse remains over by the bleachers, so I stand outside the locker room and wait. Kat doesn't mind the possibility of naked men, I guess. *Should she even be in there?*

Dylan, freshly showered, struts out in athletic pants and a long-sleeved V-neck.

He smirks when he sees me. "Hey, Mel. Kat is chatting. Surprise. Says she's going to a karaoke bar that's strict on fake IDs. I'm getting dinner if you want to join."

I clasp my hands in front of me, resisting the urge to fidget. "Only if it's at the seafood bistro. I'm allergic to all foods except lobster."

He shakes his head, hopefully in amusement, and

waves me along. I don't question Kat's desertion since it's a typical occurrence at this point. If I think too much about it, I'll get stuck in whirling doubts and sabotage anything Dylan and I have going on between us. Whatever this is, I can't have my insecurity about his sister ruin my chances with him.

I focus back on reality, stopping at the passenger side of a sleek, silver Corvette. I shut my gaping mouth as Dylan lowers himself into the car and the passenger door unlocks. My fingers linger at the handle. Dylan doesn't seem like the type of person to own a sports car; I've never seen him dress in anything nicer than jeans.

Kat has her own condo and often pays for nights out; not to mention that makeup stash in her room and Harrison's comment about country clubs. My mind puts the pieces together. *Well then. Dylan and Kat are a little richer than they let on. Don't make this a big deal. He doesn't think twice about the car he owns,* I remind myself while staring at the shiny exterior.

The window rolls down. "You getting in?" Dylan asks as I force myself from my thoughts, open the door, and sink into the leather. He points to my face as he starts the car. "Nice face paint."

A blush warms my face as I open the sun visor and check my makeup and the face paint in its mirror. I ignore the budding nerves while we nonchalantly chat about the game all the way to the nearest burger drive-in.

How romantic.

He parks at one of the drive in's outdoor menus and asks me what I want. A double patty burger, extra cheesy fries, and a large cookie dough milkshake, but I settle for a single patty and side salad. I'll remove the top bun from the burger like I always do; hopefully he won't notice. Dylan orders our food, and I shuffle through my bag for my wallet, but he waves it away. So, he's paying. Interesting. I fiddle with my fingers in my lap. *What do I want from this anyway?*

I can't lie to myself. I want to be in a relationship. That's what I've been searching for since Brady left—someone to spend time with me, go on fun dates, and have a trusted source to confine in. Dylan is the first guy to show genuine interest. That's why this matters so much. I care too much about this moment and can't ruin it like I tend to mess up everything else.

The surface-level conversation finds a lull as he sips his milkshake, and I search for the words to explain my feelings to Dylan.

He beats me to it. "So, about last night," Dylan begins.

Finally, the moment everyone has been waiting for. Drumroll, please.

I swallow, my hammering heartbeat making it difficult to speak. "I—I'm sorry. It was rather sudden, and we had a little alcohol—"

"Melanie. It's okay. No harm, no foul. You're a nice person. I have to be honest with you though." He's avoiding my gaze.

Oh, no. This was going so well. He called me nice. That's a red flag.

Dylan sighs. "I don't want you to get the wrong idea. I'm not looking for a relationship now."

My heart plummets to the car floor. "Me either," I blurt out.

"We can…see each other if you want. But not exclusive. Know what I mean?"

Basically, you want the option of having sex with me without committing to me. It's a common arrangement these days. Two can play this game. Brady moved on so why not follow his lead? Dylan gets an occasional fling, and I'll have a fair-weather companion. *Is it worth it though?* I can't meet Dylan's eyes but nod as if we hadn't made a major decision.

When I don't say anything, he sighs and grabs my trash, throwing it into the bins outside.

I ask when he returns, "Do you mind dropping me off at Kat's apartment? I left my car over there last night."

"Of course. Which reminds me…" He turns around and grabs a plastic shopping bag from the backseat. "Here's the leggings you left. I washed them."

I grab the bag from him, unable to speak. We make eye contact, unfortunately.

He studies me for a moment, his eyebrows furrowed. "We're good, right?"

"Yeah. Everything is fine," I lie. Nothing good can come from me admitting my feelings. I'll only get rejected.

He shrugs, letting me choose silence over communication, which is never a smart idea. On the way to Kat's apartment, the familiar sights of town blur by as tears gather in my eyes. I sniffle as quietly as I can and dab my eyes with my pinky. I risk a glance, but Dylan's eyes are focused on the road.

Kat's apartment lights are on as he parks his luxury sports car next to my dingy Honda in the driveway.

I mutter, "Thanks for dinner. The game was fun too." I stare at Kat's apartment and the shadowy movements behind the shades. They must be pregaming.

He unlocks the passenger door. "Anytime. I'll see you soon."

"Yeah. Sounds good."

"Have a good rest of your night, Mel—"

I step out of the car without a wave or glance behind me as I escape into my car. A few minutes pass, and he's already driven away, but I haven't moved. *Do I text him an apology? I left so abruptly. Did he think it was rude?*

But what's wrong with feeling disappointed?

Hunched over the steering wheel, I finally fit the car key into the ignition and turn it. Some sleep will help. Life has been nonstop lately, and it's starting to wear me down.

When I arrive at the dorm, Erin sits at the front desk for her weekend work shift. She peeks her eyes up from the
computer at the sound of me entering the building.

"How's it going?" Erin asks as I pass her to the stairs. She always acknowledges me when she's working. The least I can do is make small talk.

I stop and force a smile. "Great! Went to the guy's lacrosse practice game then had some dinner."

She eyes the jersey number on my face with a playful smirk. "You have friends on the team?"

"Yeah. One in particular." I slightly blush.

"Oh. Got yourself a man?"

I hesitate, trying to find the right words. "Nah. We're…talking."

"Sure, sure. So, how are classes going?"

She must have taken my hesitancy as a hint to change the subject.

"Classes. Yes, they're awesome," I lie. "You?"

"Thinking about changing my major. Not sure yet. Probably because I have a mandatory class I'm struggling with."

"You're studying…philosophy?"

"Psychology."

"Well, keep me updated on what you decide."

"Will do! Being a school counselor doesn't sound so bad. I wanna do something I enjoy. If I have to spend most of my life doing it, I want to like it."

"You do what's best for you," I encourage her though I'm a hypocrite all the same.

"You're right. Andre has been saying the same thing, except he's telling me to pray about God's plan for my life."

"Of course. Well, I'm wiped. Crazy week. See you soon," I say dismissively. I'm not in the mood to have a theological conversation about "God's plans" when I want to sleep. I'm unsure of her beliefs anyway. We've never had conversations like that before.

We say goodnight at the same time then I climb the stairs to get ready to sleep. As I lay in bed that night, the idea of switching majors takes root in my thoughts, tugging and nagging at my comfort zone. Studying something enjoyable? I let myself indulge in the idea. What kind of job would I get? Heck, what even interests me? Business is boring. I can't say I'm particularly gifted in anything except memorizing things for exams.

I've never asked myself what I want to do with my life, because it's always been assumed for me; I would take over Mom's marketing firm. The end. That's what I want, right? Safe, easy, and planned out.

Given this train of thought, what if I had a choice without failure or consequences? I think of high school, where I spent my years writing the school newspaper and yearbook; obtaining stories about everyday life without bias or a filter to make it appear prettier than it is; getting people to notice others by the power of a story and words.

If only I could fit that enjoyment for writing into the university's graduation criteria and culture's demands and expectations. Writing creatively about reality—a job I could live with every day. So, basically journalism.

My path is decided. I'll be the best businesswoman I can be and run the marketing firm like I'm supposed to, dang it.

I sigh loudly since Sophia is not in the room. Even my convictions feel false. As if I'm a photographer putting a rose-colored filter on the picture that is my life. Why do I lie to myself and accept this major as some fate? Why can't I admit the path I'm traveling on is not where I want to be?

I overthink myself to sleep, my ruminations sending me deeper into my consciousness. A dream begins. I wander a library as big as the Student Center. Book pages flutter around me, creating massive piles of paper like snow drifts. Mom stands behind me with her arms crossed, frantically pointing at her watch. A heaviness ascends over me. I turn around where Dylan laughs and beckons for me to join him in the chaos of the falling pages.

I don't remember what I choose to do.

Chapter 13

Midterms

Monday and Tuesday blur together, a hectic accumulation of homework, studying, and exams because professors thought it was a good idea to give midterms before fall break, one of the most distracting times for students. I failed the accounting midterm with a dreadful C, so hopefully it doesn't lower my overall grades. Harrison occasionally tutors me for accounting, but he can't take exams for me.

Mom's threat of removing college funding hangs over my head, a thought I avoid indulging; it makes me want to drink and forget for a while. Maybe she doesn't check my grades, and her intent was to scare me into diligence. Well, it worked. I'm terrified and filling every spare moment with my studies.

On Wednesday morning Kat and I chat about nothing important before the math midterm. Dylan enters the room and sits next to me. *Don't overthink it,* I tell myself. Dylan and my "consensual" agreement to hookup and nothing more, unfortunately, remains in effect.

He ignores Kat and says to me, "Well, Mel. The guys and I are heading to the lake for fall break. Have any plans?"

I shrug. "Study."

"It's called a break. We're finishing midterms so nothing is due."

"Didn't you know I am a certified nerd? Studying never ends. Got to keep up my reputation."

"Certified nerd? I'm the one with comics in my bedroom."

Kat gags. "Please stop doing whatever this is in front of me."

Dylan rolls his eyes, and I laugh. "What about you, Kat?" I ask.

"Going back home to party with some hometown friends."

I smile despite the sinking feeling in my chest. "Well, enjoy the shenanigans. I'll stay and be the responsible one."

The math professor runs into the classroom, apologizing about her tardiness before she even reaches the podium. She passes out the midterm, and I finish it within thirty minutes. *Not hard at all*, I think as she grades it on the spot, 97% written in red ink across the top. A sigh of relief escapes my mouth, and I cover it hoping I didn't disturb anyone working.

Someone whistles as I'm leaving the classroom for the gym. I ignore it. Surely, that's not for me. A voice calls "Melanie", so I turn my head as Harrison and Seth approach amongst the throng of students battling for space in the cramped hallway.

I wave as they catch up and stay in step with my short gait. "Hey, guys. Haven't seen you at Taco Tuesday in a while. Or you at my dorm, Seth."

Harrison shrugs. "Been busy with fraternity stuff. I'm sure I've seen you on Main." He points at his head. "But the ol' memory is fuzzy."

Seth rolls his eyes. "Your Resident Director caught me smoking weed outside your dorm with a few residents. We ran, but she stares at me every time I'm in your dorm."

I mean, it is a freshman dorm. Weird for a junior to be hanging around the girls so much, I think but I keep my judgments to myself.

Seth stops in front of me and grabs my shoulders. "We planned the most epic bar crawl over fall break. You staying in town?" he asks.

My body tenses. "Yeah. Me, myself, and I."

"Sweet. It's an unofficial Greek life event, but I consider you an honorary sister." Harrison pats my head as Seth releases me.

Why is everyone always patting my head like I'm some cute, little animal?

I ignore my irritation and give a dramatic curtsey.

"Thanks. I'm thinking about rushing in the spring."

Seth pumps his fist. "Nice. Well, meet at our place tomorrow for the beginning of the end of our short-term memory."

My plans for "studying"–getting lost in a book or working out anything to ignore the stress of college. Surely, I could find something else to do with my free time this extended weekend other than partying.

I don't mind the invitation. Better to be invited than ignored or ditched.

~ ~ ~

On Thursday evening–after a long day of trying to fill my time with anything other than school–I'm on the fraternity's front step like an obedient canine begging for pets and a treat. *That's why everyone has a compulsion to pat my head. I'm so docile.* I text Harrison that I'm here and lean on the looming white columns.

Every girl passing me is dressed to the nines, their shimmery, sleek outfits causing me to stand out with my faux leather skirt and cropped long sleeve shirt. *No matter what I do, I don't look like them. What am I missing?* I tug at the skirt's hem. Kat picked out this outfit for me, but I don't feel comfortable in it. My feet ache from these high high heels already.

Seth rescues me from the porch before my mind spirals and sabotages the night before it begins.

His eyes slowly travel up and down my body.

"Looking fine tonight. Harrison is grabbing drinks for us," Seth explains as we wind around people leaving for the night and into his room.

Strangers crowd Seth's room, so I sit on his scratchy fabric couch. He soon joins me, a lit joint in hand. I try not to inhale the stench as I adjust my outfit.

"He's bringing the good stuff tonight. His uncle bought him this fancy vodka in celebration of Harrison getting that finance internship. Said he was saving it for a special occasion, but we convinced him tonight was the right time," Seth says as he leans closer to me, our shoulders touching.

"Why doesn't he buy another one?" I ask, shifting in my seat, so I can put a few inches between us.

Seth snorts, a whisp of smoke rising to the ceiling. "Vodka over $200? With what money?"

"Oh. He mentioned country clubs…"

"Harrison? Rich? Ahh, he tricked you too."

I furrow my eyebrows. That's not the charming Harrison I know.

Seth puts his bare feet onto the chipped coffee table. "His family was rich at some point. But the recession a few years back sent his dad's company into bankruptcy. They used the rest of their money to keep up appearances. His stuff is hand me downs and old models. Ever see his car?" When I don't answer he continues. "Didn't think so. It's old and run down. He walks or carpools. People buy him drinks because he's Harrison."

Seth stretches, relaxing deeper into the couch as he ridicules his frat brother. "He's smoke and mirrors. Anything to make himself look good."

"When did he tell you this?" I'm in denial.

Seth holds up his joint. "A little bit of weed will make anyone chill enough to talk about their struggles. Even the most prideful."

The revelation swirls through my head. That's why Harrison sells papers to Seth and probably other students and explains why he tries to sell me pills for focus. He's keeping up the appearance of being well-off for his own reasons.

Even the most enchanting people have secrets.

Harrison strides in with the expensive booze, everyone cheering as he holds up the glass bottle. A grin lights up his whole face at the applause and adoration. He pours the vodka into red solo cups and distributes them, the liquid burning all the way down my throat as usual. My thoughts of his deceptiveness disappear.

I don't want to think for a while.

Seth hauls a carload of giggling young adults to Main. Harrison sits up front, the car ride's DJ, as everyone but me poorly raps along to a song on the radio. They roll the windows down, so fresh air fills the car and gives the noise somewhere to escape.

The streets bustle with more occupants than usual,

because of the prolonged weekend and the Octoberfest themes each bar is advertising for more patrons as if their business struggles in a college town. I stumble after the group, my heels finding every dip and crack in the cobblestone sidewalk. Seth hangs back, grabs my hand, and drags me forward to everyone else; thankfully I don't break an ankle.

"Catch us if you can," Harrison calls to me from the front of the group.

I roll my eyes, paying closer attention to my steps. Tonight, I'll focus on the present moment, not my insecurities of partying with Greek life; not stress from school and life; not my insistent thoughts wandering to Dylan, wondering what he's doing tonight and who he is with. If Dylan can go out and do whatever he wants, so can I.

The first bar we enter is some pub I've never been to before; it's no different than the others with its low lighting, fluorescents signs, and tables haphazardly scattered throughout the establishment. I order some fruity beer that Dylan likes and stand in a circle with some of the sorority girls that rode in the car with us. *What do I say to them?*

Like a godsend, Jessica strolls into the bar. She runs over, waving and hugging people whose names I don't remember. *Too many people, too many names.*

Jessica turns to me. "Your outfit is so cute. You've

been shopping obviously."

"Yeah, I haven't seen you in the bathroom lately," I joke.

Jessica laughs. "Moved out." She nudges a girl next to her. "And into a campus house with this one and another sister named Lauren. Are you joining us for the spring semester?"

"Of course. It seems like so much fun," I reply, eyeing the others and hoping to connect with them on some level; some nod, but that's all they give me.

The sorority girls sway to the music with their drinks and have conversations without me, so I lean against a wall, watching. There's a coiling in the pit of my stomach, screaming with the need to blend in with everyone else. Aren't I doing it right—going out, wearing these clothes, and drinking until I can't remember? I want to fit in, not be the person who always gets butted out of conversations and must fight to be included. Being myself didn't work but neither does mimicking them.

What am I doing wrong?

They disappear into the bathroom, so I order another beer and search for Harrison and Seth. They sit in a circular booth at the front of the pub with others, smoking cigarettes. Pulling up a bar stool, I listen to them banter about the stock market; their words mean nothing to me. So, I sip my beer and survey the pub and its occupants. *I wish Dylan was here. Wait, no. He chose to be elsewhere, and I am here tonight.* I need to focus on the present.

So, the impossible yet again.

Harrison and Seth finish smoking and their financial discussions. We depart from the pub without the sorority girls we brought with us and hustle to the next bar across the street, which is a restaurant with a rooftop club. The first-floor restaurant appears to be a classy place with its white tablecloths and polished mahogany floor. It's closed, but the winding stairs open to a semi-roofed club. Harrison heads to the bar and returns with vodka cranberries, passing them to Seth and me.

"I know the bartender. This one is on the house." Harrison cheers as we tap our plastic cups together and drink. "Now the real party can begin!"

We drain our free cups of liquor down our throats, Harrison and Seth disappearing into the crowd while I step onto the dance floor until I'm lost in it. The crowd is one, mingling into a mass of repressed stress and regret. The more I drink, and drink I do, the more I don't care. My feet tip over cups on the floor, the lights bouncing off the spilled liquor and create a rainbow below me. *I'm walking on rainbows.*

I spot Harrison leaving the dance floor at one point during the night, so I accompany him to the benches bordering the room.

"What's wrong?" I stumble over my tongue and lips.

Harrison clutches a cup, his wide eyes scanning the

crowd. "I saw her. She's here." His mouth moves more, but the music and my intoxicated state make it impossible to understand him.

I follow his gaze to a particularly stunning woman, her dark hair hanging in a loose ponytail down her back; she's fit and skinny but has obtained the curves that everyone is jealous of. She hangs onto some guy– wait, is that Isaac– and the crowd whirls around her, the pinnacle of the dance floor.

That must be Lauren.

Somewhere deep down I know that's who Dylan had in his room the other night. I stare at her a little longer, recognizing her as the one who helped me with the clothing dilemma my first night out. My smile disappears in the wake of her magnetic confidence. *Why in the world would Dylan ever turn her down? Why would he be with me if he can have that?*

Seth staggers off the dance floor. "Let's go smoke," he begs. His voice snaps me out of my reverie, my attention returning to Harrison who remains incoherent. Seth pulls him by the arm, and I become their shadow, giving one last glance at Lauren. She's on the pole in the middle of the floor, swirling around like an acrobatic ballerina.

Of course, she can pole dance.

My mind shifts back to the problem in front of me. This is the first time I've been around a truly intoxicated

Harrison. Turns out he's a raging, sad drunk. I notice his bloodshot eyes and puffy face while we settle him into the car; he whines about Lauren and the "cruelty that is life". As if a doctor, Seth grabs the medicine from the center counsel: pre-rolled blunts. Without hesitation Seth lights them up, handing one to Harrison. They leave the car windows rolled up, the smoke and stench swirling around me. I stretch out in the backseat, staring at the ceiling with liquor swirling in my body and the marijuana tickling my nose.

Harrison eventually falls quiet. Both guys puff at their blunts, accepting whatever good feeling is washing over them. My stomach growls, and a stillness descends over me. Any more thoughts of Lauren–and the fact she was with Isaac–come to a halt.

"You try smoking yet?" Seth asks.

"Nah." I can't say much else, my tongue heavy in my mouth.

Harrison sighs deeply. "You'll have to come over and smoke with us."

Seth gestures with his blunt. "Big group. Different color skin, beliefs, all of that. No hate. Just love. We're human in the end, ya know."

What a wonderful idea. People being able to exist in a space with different opinions but without hate. Right in the car, I promise myself that I will try to contribute to accepting everyone's differences and promoting peace.

Sounds like a marvelous idea.

I open the car door to puke.

Seth drives us back to the frat house, and I pass out on Harrison's futon. The morning finds me ruminating on how Seth shouldn't have driven the car. I lift my head up from the futon to see Seth curled up in a large reclining chair. Harrison is sprawled on his bed, shirtless and in his underwear; I blush at the sight and look away.

At least we made it back without any trouble.

On Friday night we are at the club. I'm standing at the bar about to order a drink when some guy approaches from the front of the club. He acknowledges me and asks the bartender for two shots.

"Hey. I'm Matthew. And you are?"

I clear my throat. "Melanie."

He hands me the shot, and we don't break eye contact as we kick them back down our throats.

"You go to school around here?" Matthew asks as we lean against the bar.

"Yeah, the university here. You?"

He grins. "Community college. I think I've seen you around a few times."

"Well, I'm glad I'm noticeable." I cringe at my own words. *Desperate much?*

"Want to sit somewhere more private?"

I agree, he orders another drink for each of us, then leads me to a more secluded booth. We talk over the music, leaning in close as we talk about school and our hometowns.

Seth stumbles over, using our table to steady himself.

"Gonna smoke. You coming?"

I glance at Matthew then back to Seth and shake my head. "No, I'll stay here."

"A friend of yours?" Matthew asks when Seth stalks away.

I shrug. "Kinda?"

We talk and drink, drink and talk until time doesn't exist anymore. Eventually, we wind up in a cab to his place. He shows me around, and the tour ends in his bedroom. My legs give out, my vision blacking out for a moment, but he's behind me, helping me back to my feet. The giggling pouring from my mouth doesn't stop even when I lay down on his bed.

An image of Dylan darts through my mind. Then Brady. And that's all. Things are blurry. I'm vaguely aware of everything Matthew and I do, the details flying around my head, refusing to become concrete memories. This night is a haze of booze, kisses, and other things before I descend into chaotic dreams mirroring the same.

~ ~ ~

The sunlight hits my eyes, and I startle awake, alone in someone's bed. I brush my hair back from my face, a headache making it nearly impossible to open my eyes. *Oh, yes. Matthew. The guy from the bar.* I crawl out of bed to find a bathroom. It's Saturday afternoon, and I have no idea where I am.

Matthew is not home, nor did he leave a note. I sit on his couch and scroll through my phone, wondering who I can call. Kat won't be in town until Sunday. I think of Dylan, guilt rushing to my face in a blush. He's not in town either. I try to call Harrison and Seth, but they don't pick up. With a sigh, I try one more person. The phone rings on the other end and a voice comes through.

"Hello?"

"Hi, Erin. It's Melanie. This is super embarrassing, but I don't have my car. I'm at some guy's house. He's not here. I don't know the address, and I'm broke so I don't want to order a cab. Wait. Are you on campus—"

Erin's laughter interrupts me. "I got you. I stayed over break. Share your location with me on your phone, and I'll be there." Her voice becomes muffled as if she's talking to someone. Then she says, "Andre and I got breakfast and we're hanging out. My car is at the autobody shop, so we can pick you up in his truck. Hope you don't mind."

"Not at all. Thanks so much." I end the call.

I do mind. I could have called Andre because he's volunteered to pick me up multiple times, but this circumstance is too personal to ask someone who's a Christian; won't he have something to say about me hooking up with someone? I blush knowing he'll be in the car with us.

I need a ride, so I'll take my chances.

I send my location to Erin's phone. Heels in hand, I walk outside, my bare feet accepting the cold air and concrete. Like a child in timeout, my butt finds the curb.

Why do I feel bad about this? Because I was reckless and slept with a stranger? Because I was drunk and wasn't in control? Matthew could have been some psycho killer luring unaware women to his apartment.

I better be more careful.

Andre parks his truck in front of me fifteen minutes later; enough time for me to rot in mental turmoil. I open the door and climb into the back seat, avoiding eye contact with them.

Andre begins driving, and Erin turns to me from the front seat. "Hey, you okay? He do something he wasn't supposed to?"

I shake my head, a blush creeping onto my face. "I was drunk and…" I watch Andre through the rearview mirror, but he doesn't take his eyes from the road, his right arm resting on the middle seat that's been pulled down.

I clear my throat. "…and I'm emotional about it, and I don't know why."

Erin's scrunched eyebrows relax. "That makes sense. If it's a new thing, it might feel confusing. I'm making sure you're good. Didn't know if we needed to beat someone up." She half-heartedly chuckles; we know what could have happened, but no one wants to talk about that.

Andre catches my frequent glances at him in the rearview. He clears his throat. "You don't have to keep looking at me like that, Melanie."

"Like what?"

"Like you've been a bad kid and I'm judging your choices."

"Well, you're a Christian—"

"Which means I have standards, but I'm not perfect. I don't expect you to live like me."

"What do you mean?"

He shrugs, his eyes never leaving the road. "You don't have the same convictions…beliefs that I do. If you aren't a Christian, why would I expect you to act like one?"

Andre sighs at my silence and reiterates, "We want to make sure you're okay. That's all."

I cradle one knee to my chest and rest my chin on it. "I'll be alright. Thanks for picking me up." My stomach immediately grumbles. Andre and Erin laugh, my awkwardness and shame diminishing in the light-hearted moment.

"Sounds like it's lunch time. Where to?" he asks.

Without hesitation Erin throws up her hands and yells, "Tacos!"

No one argues with that, so Andre drives to the local taco joint. They settle into a sports-related conversation, so I take the chance to process. Okay, what are the facts? I slept with a stranger. I don't have to tell Dylan about this weekend. We aren't in that kind of relationship. I didn't cheat on Dylan. It's simple, right?

The festering remorse doesn't help.

We order our food, and I eat my taco salad bowl with them at the dorm in the first-floor lounge. It's larger than the other lounges and has a television, several sets of couches, and a massive dining room table for group study sessions and projects.

Andre stretches. "Well, we're going to play some multiplayer video games for a bit. You busy?"

"Sounds like fun. I have some homework to catch up on," I lie.

I excuse myself right after my belligerent lie. Midterms mean a reprieve from the constant assignments, but they don't question it. They say goodbye as I escape to my room. I want to be alone, to drown in my thoughts like I do so well. My empty room welcomes me, and I flop onto the warm bed.

A text pops up on my screen: "One more night, one more bar crawl. See ya tonight."

It's from Seth. *When did he get my number?*

He's right. It's Saturday, and the Greek life bar crawl has one more night to attend. It won't look good when I rush if I don't show up for the last night, right? Gotta finish what I started.

Who needs feelings? I have people to impress tonight.

Later that evening I'm back at the fraternity for pregaming in Harrison's room. Harrison and Seth don't ask where I ended up last night or how I got home. *They aren't your mom. They don't have to keep tabs on you. But it seems like a common curtsy to me.* I rub my temples, my back-and-forth thoughts giving me a headache, or it's the constant liquor I've had for two days straight.

I throw back a whisky shot then join Seth in his car, everyone piling in around me; there are more people than seats. Tonight's agenda—make a good impression. They must like me, so they'll allow me in their sorority next semester.

Seth miraculously finds parking; the streets of Main are as crowded on Saturday as they were the last two nights. Ballet flats cover my feet, so I walk ahead of the girls in their towering heels. Harrison leads us to the rooftop bar, even as the wind nips at my short black skirt. My nylon tights and the bar's outdoor heaters provide some comfort from the cold.

We sip our drinks at the edge of the raging dance floor near a blazing heater. Between sips of liquor, I ask about upcoming Greek life events and laugh along with their shameless gossip about people I don't know. They order more drinks and strut to the dance floor. I join them then we lose ourselves in the deafening noise and strobing lights.

Between the drinks, dancing, and bathroom breaks, hours pass by the time a drunken Harrison leans against me as we stagger along the sidewalk with Seth to his car. Seth hands Harrison a blunt which Harrison obediently smokes. I expect Seth to light up his own, but he starts the car and drives into the dark night.

Where are we, I wonder as factory buildings appear on either side of us. Seth stops the vehicle on a street void of cars, and he revs the engine. My heart palpitates, beating wildly in response.

This is new. I don't like new.

"What are you doing?" I ask Seth, my voice not much louder than a whisper.

In response, the car accelerates, screeching from the abrupt press on the gas pedal. I fall back into the seat, scrambling to lock in my seatbelt, my sweating hands making it impossible. Harrison throws his arms up and giggles as if he's on a carnival ride. Seth's foot doesn't let off the pedal as the car surges forward.

"Please, slow down. What if someone—" I plead but the car propels itself further down the street.

Massive light poles and parked semis come at us and pass at an alarming rate, so I squeeze my eyes shut, clutching the seat with feet braced on the floor. *We're going to run out of road.* I hear myself begging Seth to stop while he and Harrison holler like this is some sort of game.

I open my eyes as the car tires screech. Seth turns the

wheel, the car drifting in the cul-de-sac. My side slams into the door regardless of the seatbelt, the breath knocked out of me. Tiny black spots flutter in my vision as I take a shaky breath.

Seth straightens the car, and it comes to an abrupt stop. He turns to me, tears from laughter running down his ruddy cheeks. "Should have seen your face!"

Harrison pipes in, his voice slow and dragging, "The car goes fast. Nothing to worry about."

"Not the first time we've done this here. We survived," Seth justifies, as if their excuses make me feel any better.

The only response I can muster is a nod as the adrenaline dissipates and my body becomes heavy and numb. I sink into the seat, rubbing my elbow which took the brunt of the impact with the door. *That will bruise.* Between the liquor, the stench of weed swirling through the car, and Seth's antics, my thoughts are slow and unattached to the situation.

"Well, I'll be a gentleman tonight. I'll drive you back to your dorm," Seth says as he accelerates away from the factories.

A pain erupts in my stomach. Sweat beads on my forehead. When the dorm is in sight, I nearly fall to the concrete as I stumble out the door before the car stops at the curb. I collapse onto the cool tiles of the first floor's public bathroom and heave anything left in my stomach into the toilet.

What a way to end my first Greek life bar crawl weekend—puking and without confirmation if the sororities are willing to let me join next semester. I didn't secure anyone's phone number or invitations to hang out with them, not even Jessica.

What a waste of a weekend.

Now that I'm alone, I allow myself to recall Seth not listening to me in the car. This pervasive feeling crawls up my arms, constricting my parched throat, while one word echoes in my mind over and over.

Unsafe.

Unsafe.

Unsafe.

Chapter 14

Sunday Of Fall Break

A throbbing headache forces my eyes open. I turn over and groan at the sight of the clock; it's only 7 a.m. No use trying to sleep in on the weekend anymore. To pass time, I browse my phone, mindlessly watching the highlights of everyone's fall break: the pregaming, the dancing, and bonfires. This eats up an hour, but I can't ignore my achy body any longer; I begrudgingly roll out of bed. Snatching half a bagel from my food basket, a water bottle, and the cream cheese container from the mini fridge, I head for the lounge. A toaster resides in every lounge since they aren't allowed in our rooms.

Can't trust young adults with unsupervised toasters, I suppose.

With my phone in one hand and the toasted bagel in the other, I sit on a lounge chair and continue scrolling between bites, unsure how else to fill my time before classes tomorrow. *I can start this week's homework assignments to get ahead. Will that alleviate this stress?*

The scrolling brings me to a picture that Jessica posted last night from the bar crawl, and my mind inevitably wanders to Harrison and Seth. A knot ties itself in my stomach at the memory. What's my hesitation about? People joy ride all the time.

A message pops up on my phone: "Call me when you can. Important."

From Mom.

My stomach drops. She's left me alone most of the semester, preoccupied with her marketing firm and finalizing the divorce with Dad. I devour the rest of the bagel, not giving my thoughts time to spiral to worst-case scenarios. My fingers shake as I press her contact on the screen, and the phone starts ringing. I hold the phone to my ear as she exclaims from the other line, "Wow, that was quick!"

I swallow. "I was holding my phone when you texted. Had to finish eating my bagel."

She clicks her tongue. "Can't do carbs for breakfast, Honey. Bad for your blood sugar. I started drinking bone broth when I wake up. So good for you." She pauses, taking a sip of said bone broth. "Unwanted curves run on my side of the family."

"You don't let me forget," I say, trying to ignore her advice. I glance down at my thighs. It's not the first time she's mentioned this; quite the usual comment in my household while growing up.

Mom and her sisters never let me forget it.

She clears her throat, bringing me back to reality. "Okay. Down to business. I've been watching your grades this semester."

"Yeah. I did well on my midterms." Of course, I don't mention the C in accounting. I elaborate for her sake, "They aren't in the system yet."

"We made an agreement. You would keep A's this semester to get into the honor's society and other academic opportunities. You're not holding up your end of the deal."

"But the semester isn't over. I promise I'll get them up. They don't decide about the honor society until your final grades at the end—" My heart starts its familiar racing.

She sighs, interrupting me. "I'm not sure what you're doing. These are basic classes. You shouldn't be hovering so close to C's even at midterms. What is happening in accounting?"

"Please give me until the end of the semester."

"I think you might need some encouragement to study harder." Her meaning is too clear. Memories from high school resurface of when she wouldn't let me go out with friends if I got a bad grade on a test; punishment would surely "encourage" me to try harder next time.

This is one of the worst-case scenarios my brain dreaded.

She delivers the final blow. "I'll have to cut you off. We can talk about it once your final grades are posted at the end of the semester."

The world spins around me. I clutch the chair's arm to steady my shaking body.

"You'll want to get another job to make up the difference. The monthly payment for the semester is due at the end of each month. I'll change the automatic payment to your bank account for October—"

I don't hear anything else she says because my breath lost its natural rhythm and my pounding heart echoes in my ears, harsh and all-consuming.

I mutter, "Gotta go. Talk to you later."

Somehow, I make it back to my room and in bed before the crying starts. My nerves have taken over; my breath trapped somewhere in my chest instead of exhaling. Financial stress always loomed above me, so I worked every summer to save, to alleviate the impending financial burden known as college; my scholarship was supposed to help too. Even that wasn't enough for everything. There's the car payment and insurance. Gas. Groceries. Phone. Textbooks. Room and board. Now the cost of my classes, which are separate from my school loans increasing from interest.

At least she pays for medical insurance. I don't trust her to keep doing that either.

How long do I lay in bed, curled into myself and

numb? I don't know. Students return to the dorm from break—shutting doors, running feet, laughter, and muddled conversations. Someone knocks on the bathroom door.

"One moment," I squeak. I sit up, dabbing my eyes with a tissue and pulling my blanket around me. I appear sick, right? My puffy eyes and sniffling won't betray me.

"Come in!" I call.

Erin opens the door and sticks her head through. "Hey you! How was your—Oh! You not feeling good?"

I clear my throat, hoping that it helps my case. "Yeah, I think the stress from midterms caught up to me," I tell her as she stands in the doorway wearing mismatched socks.

"Aww, I'm sorry. Do you need anything? I can get you soup for old time's sake."

I shake my head. "No, I bought a salad from the school's new convenient market, store, whatever it's called."

"Darn. A small group of us are watching the college football game down in the lounge. Maybe next time. Feel better soon!" She leaves with a wave and slowly shuts the bathroom door.

I sigh, the initial shock settling, my brain foggy from crying and my lingering hangover. *Now what? How can I come up with that money every month?* Instead of finding an answer, I sink into bed and close my eyes. My thoughts come to a standstill. The world disappears. The inevitable dreams find me, but they are as dark as my mind; unclear but ominous all the same.

I wake with a start, the clock and my stomach telling me its dinnertime. Ignoring my absent appetite, I grab the salad from the fridge and sit in my desk chair, staring at the leafy greens and soggy chicken.

My thoughts are impossible to ignore. Why don't I open up and share my struggles with someone? It's a simple solution to my stress. *I can't tell Kat. I can almost predict her sarcastic reply.* I continue down a mental list of names. Hayley and Alex usually give advice or a positive outlook. I need something else right now. Comfort? Understanding?

An image of Dylan flashes through my mind as well, but our conversations remain surface level. Sharing my struggles with him feels like crossing some unstated boundary.

My mind wanders to Erin. She has always been nice to me for no apparent reason. *Why do I lie to her? Not even once, but on multiple occasions!* And Andre. He's always ready for the rescue, making sure inebriated me makes it to her room in one piece. Why didn't I accept their invitations to hang out this weekend? I can't find an answer to that.

So, I eat alone in my room, my thoughts unceasing. Loneliness coils itself into my chest like a friendly companion, so I curl up in bed with it; it's my own fault. Too many emotions tonight, and I don't have answers. If I don't figure it out, I'll have a drink and pretend I'm okay a while longer.

I'm not the only one feeling this way. I can't be.

Chapter 15

Mid-November

The rest of October and November slip away; I forget it's Thanksgiving break until professors mention it in class at the beginning of the week. I text Mom telling her, "I was too busy with homework to drive home", and she replies with "okay". Holidays have lost their grandeur since my parents' split and impending divorce; Mom doesn't do much other than work nowadays, and Dad usually can't afford to cook anything significant. *I don't want to see her either*, I think; the anger for cutting me off before the end of the semester hasn't abated. She gave me no warning.

At least I had enough money left in savings to pay October's class bill.

That dreaded conversation with Mom over finances and a good crying session–or two–led me to scouring job websites for a retail job. Thankfully, a thrift store was hiring for part-time help. Now I tediously balance my waking hours between classes, the gym, my two part-time jobs, homework, and partying whenever Kat or Dylan invite me out; I avoid driving anywhere with Harrison and Seth but hang out with them if they approach me while I'm out.

My already stretched thin time is divided even further. I'm not stressed. The distress isn't bubbling and never settling. I'm fine.

Even I can't convince myself of my own lie.

Wednesday afternoon classes and a gym session come and go, and afterwards I lay on my bed listening to Sophia–yes, she exists–and Erin chat in the bathroom about their favorite Thanksgiving foods while they pack for the extended weekend. My headache burrows deeper into my skull, leaving me distant from their conversation. I reply to Erin's question that I am staying over break. Some residential staff will be here, so the dorms will remain open for people like me who don't want to go home and the international students that can't.

Soon after announcing these plans to Erin, my phone rings. Dylan's name appears on the screen, my heart racing in tandem. Why would he call me? Shouldn't he be going home for the holiday? Possibilities run through my head, all of which are worst-case scenarios. *Oh, I should answer.*

I swipe the phone and stammer, "Hi. Uh—What's up?" My mouth is dry. I grab my water bottle, swallowing as quietly as I can.

"Long time no see. No, That's a bad joke. It's only

been a few hours since class." He clears his throat. "So, you mentioned not having any Thanksgiving plans."

"You do listen when I talk. What a relief." Hopefully my banter makes me sound more causal than I feel.

"Well, do you want to go with me and Kat to my grandparents' lake house?"

The lake house he went to for fall break belongs to his family. I was not expecting that.

My heartrate settles as I consider my options. To my dismay, Dylan and I remain in the same messing-around-without-any-commitment agreement, so this is a new development. It's a little more personal. But I don't want to stay at school on a holiday, and there will be free food. It could be fun meeting their family too. Stay here alone or go to a lake house with friends for a weekend?

"How long do I have to pack?" I ask surprised by my own boldness.

"I can buy you thirty minutes before Kat starts cussing me out."

I laugh. "Okay. I'll text you when I'm done packing."

Kat swears in the background. Dylan shushes her and says, "Great. See you soon."

I hang up and scramble around my room, stuffing trip necessities into an overnight bag. *Look at me now. Accepting spontaneous plans and not getting overwhelmed.*

Maybe I'm in my character-development arc.

Erin pokes her head in from the bathroom door,

watching my mad dash around the room.

She laughs. "I have never seen you move so fast sober. Have Thanksgiving plans?"

I turn to her and nod, unable to hide the silly grin on my face. "Dylan is inviting me over for Thanksgiving."

"The lacrosse player? For a holiday? I thought you two were casual." She crosses her arms, a playful gleam in her eyes.

"I know. I know. Trying not to read too much into it but…" My initial excitement begins to bow to the inevitable wave of unanswered questions and nerves.

She interrupts the impending flood of insecurity saying, "Well, try and enjoy yourself. You deserve some relaxation."

"You're right. I'm going to try to enjoy it." I grab my pillow and place my book into my purse. "Have a Happy Thanksgiving! And safe travels," I say.

"You too. Happy Thanksgiving!"

We simultaneously wave as she shuts the door. With the packing done, I text Dylan and walk downstairs to the lobby. I scroll on my phone until a familiar sports car honks at me. Wiping my sweaty hands on my sweatpants, I scoop up my things and jump into the back seat.

Punk rock music greets me from the car's speakers. Dylan smirks from the driver's seat, our eyes briefly meeting in the rearview mirror. I wave at Kat, but she doesn't acknowledge me. *I don't think she saw me,* I reassure myself.

"Welcome aboard. I'm about to whisk you away to the countryside. Please excuse the winding roads," Dylan says as we drive away, the campus soon behind us.

"Yeah, he drives like a grandpa, so try not to fall asleep," Kat mutters as she props her legs on the dash.

Dylan slams a fist on the steering wheel, and I jump.

Kat throws her arms up. "You're so sensitive. It was a joke."

"I've asked you not to comment on my driving. Multiple times. You know it makes me nervous. And put your legs down." He sighs, and I watch as his grip loosens on the wheel. "I want to enjoy this weekend with the family. You could try too."

Kat huffs, turning her head to the window and placing her feet on the floor in response. Dylan adjusts the music, drowning out any chance at reconciliation or conversation. I lean back into my seat trying to make myself comfortable. I've never seen Dylan show that much emotion to something seemingly trivial. They have bickered plenty of times, but this felt different, like the joke struck a painful place for Dylan.

Clues about Dylan and Kat's life beyond this campus won't be able to hide this weekend.

I'll be Melanie Holmes for a few days.

I gaze out the window and watch the scenery blur past us. My mind loses itself in the growing forest around us as Dylan weaves the car along the zig-zagging roads. Worries begin to blend with the shadows creeping at the edge of the tree line. For a moment, I notice my breathing. In and out, chest and stomach expanding and contracting, concentration pinned on this one action. My thoughts are not this listless waterfall of to-do lists and responsibilities. This weekend ahead is dedicated time with friends, not the constant stress of college life.

Silence between Dylan and Kat permeates the entire trip, even during a bathroom stop halfway to our destination. I let the quiet ensue, munching on gas station trail mix and distracting myself with Dylan's road trip playlist and the scenery.

Slivers of the lake begin revealing itself between the pine trees. Dylan drives through an open gate into a lakeside community and turns the car into a spacious winding driveway ending at a house. His grandparents' lake house—no, their lake mansion—stands a considerable distance from its neighbors on the right and left. Cars and minivans line the driveway. My stomach drops. *How many people are here?*

As if an answer to my unvoiced question, a crowd pours out of the house, filling the wrap around porch as Dylan parks the car near the garage as if they intentionally left a spot for his car. They swarm Kat and Dylan as they exit the car, rattling their pleasantries and kissing each other's cheeks. This is more than immediate family. There are aunts, uncles, their spouses, cousins, and children many of which are clad in different designer labels.

I lean against the car with my thrifted travel bag, trying to disappear. *I'm a friend, nothing more.*

Nothing more.

An older woman with black hair and dimples approaches me, holding her arms out. "You must be Melanie. Dylan mentioned you would be joining us. I'm their Mama, but I'm Monica to you. No need to be formal." She wraps her arms around me in a quick, encompassing hug.

"Thank you for your hospitality." They're the only words I can find with all the laughter and conversation distracting me.

Her smile never falters. "Of course. You're more than welcome here." She makes a noise in her throat, getting Dylan's attention. "Dylan, why don't you show Melanie to a room?"

He grabs his bag from the car, takes mine from my clenched hands, and motions his head for me to follow him. The families flow back into the massive house behind us, Kat somewhere in the sea of unfamiliar faces. Dylan leads me through a towering entry way, past a grand kitchen, and through hallways lined with family pictures and painted portraits of the lake.

At the beginning of one hallway, he enters a room where a few sets of bunk beds cram the space. Dylan sets our bags on a bright blue folding chair and turns to me.

"Well, I pulled some strings, so we have this room to ourselves. Kat has her own room because of her insomnia. Hope you don't mind the bunks."

"This is great." I set my pillow and messenger bag on a bottom bunk. *Kat has insomnia. Well, that's one thing I didn't know before.*

He bites the inside of his cheeks. "I should have told you about the whole family being here. Didn't want to give you a reason to say no."

"It will be nice to meet everyone. Don't expect me to remember names and how they relate to you."

"I am quizzing you after—"

Kat interrupts from the open door. "Dinner in fifteen minutes."

I give her a thumbs up, and she disappears without another word. I freshen up in the bathroom, taming my wavy hair with a comb and changing out of my traveling clothes into a knitted gray sweater and leggings. *Everyone was already dressed so nicely. Hopefully there isn't a dress code for dinner*, I think as I survey myself in the full-length mirror.

Dylan smirks from the bathroom doorway, tastefully appraising my outfit choice. As if reading my thoughts, he says, "I like to rebel too. They can keep the fancy clothes. I'll indulge in the nice car and tuition."

We walk to the dining room, well, more like dining

hall. The ceiling stretches upward ending at a shimmering glass chandelier. A wooden table dominates the right side of the room while temporary tables are set up for the influx of bodies. Dylan shows me to a seat near who I presume to be his grandparents; they don't seem too old, but their slight wrinkles give them away. Dylan sits on my right, Kat to the left, his grandparents, and Monica in front of me.

Don't mess this up, Melanie.

The table boasts several charcuterie boards brimming with varieties of meats, breads, cheeses, fruits, and dips; full wine bottles occupy any empty space. Everyone helps themselves to the feast, piling their porcelain plates and filling the room with idle chatter. Dylan pours me a glass of ruby red wine then one for himself. It's refreshing without the too sugary aftertaste of some wines I've tried at Kat's place.

Their grandma addresses me first. "Dylan brought someone new this year. Will you introduce her?" She raises her eyebrows at Dylan.

He's mid-bite so I answer. "I'm Melanie. I am a…classmate. Thank you for your hospitality—"

She cuts me off with a wave of her hand. "It is no problem. We are blessed, so we share that with others. Glad to have you here, Melanie. You may call me Greta." She smiles and sips the wine. "I hope you enjoy the wine. It's one of my favorite blends from our vineyards."

Coughing to keep myself from choking on the grape I just ate, I side-eye Dylan who shrugs. Kat stares at her plate, unfazed at the mention of her family's source of riches. *Who in the world forgets to mention their family owns wine vineyards? That's so cool!*

I sputter, "Oh, they never mentioned…"

Their grandpa clicks his tongue. "Sounds like your kids, Monica. Not mentioning the family business that gives them their stuff."

Monica bites her lower lip then screws her face into a grin. "Your own kids are carrying on the family business."

"Yeah, we are so grateful. Obviously," Kat comments as she heaps more food on her plate and pours another glass of wine.

Their grandpa pushes up his glasses. "My grandparents immigrated to this country to farm and make wine. Built a more than comfy living for everyone. Family members should contribute." He shrugs as if it's a straightforward concept.

"Pa, why don't we table this conversation for another time? We have a guest," Monica insists, her voice steady despite the rising tension.

Greta chimes in, "Ernesto, they attend college, and Kat is going to be a professional swimmer."

Kat slams down her glass of wine, the liquid sloshing over the sides.

"I already told you. I'm no longer swimming, *Nonna*.

Sorry that I can't live up to the family expectation of greatness."

The room goes quiet for a moment as Kat shoves her chair behind her; she storms off into the maze of hallways. Ernesto clicks his tongue, and everyone resumes eating and drinking as if this is a typical occurrence. I glance around the dining room, but no one moves to check on her. Dylan scowls at his wine glass while Monica picks at her food.

Grabbing a napkin, I wipe up the spilled wine and say to no one in particular, "Thank you for the meal. I'll check on her if that's alright." I slowly stand and push in my chair.

Hopefully Kat will make enough noise to direct me to her room. I wander the house, peeking into every open door until I pass the bunk room and hear someone at the end of the hall.

"Wanted to see how you were doing," I announce at the open door, waiting for permission to enter.

"Don't be so polite. Come in," she replies.

I step into the room where Kat sits at a vanity applying concealer to her face.

I swallow, searching for words. "I'm sor—"

Kat sighs. "I swear, if you apologize..." She turns to me. "Now you understand why I don't come home. They're all patronizing as fu—"

"Why did you stop swimming?"

For once, Kat doesn't answer right away. I lean against the door frame while she finishes the concealer. She sets it down, and the bottle clatters against the vanity's glass top. Right when I think she'll drop the subject, she clears her throat. She picks up a brush and blush pallet, flicking the lid open.

"Me. I didn't take it seriously. I had a swimming scholarship, a spot on the college team that could get me into professional swimming someday. And I blew it," Kat admits. She glowers at the mirror for a long moment. "I screwed it up like I screw everything up."

This is the first time Kat has shown any sort of self-contempt. Fragments of positive affirmations fly through my brain, but what would help her at this moment? I rub the sides of my head, wanting something useful to come out of my mouth. Before I utter anything, she stands up from the leather stool.

"No use crying about it." She dabs her fingers below her eyes and grabs her purse from the floor. "Nothing good lasts, right?" Kat pushes past me, pathetically frozen by the door. "Going to a friend's house. Don't miss me."

And she's gone without inviting me.

I get it. I'm underage but that never deters my participation in Taco Tuesdays and her dragging me to bars and clubs that aren't strict on minors. This isn't the first time, or the last I suspect, that she'll decline inviting me. How can someone be so inclusive but also exclusive?

I stand a moment longer, all the information I gained this evening swirling around in my head. With a sigh, I return to the bunk room. The tense atmosphere in that dining room is enough for me tonight.

I change into pajamas and settle into the comfy folding chair with my book. Reading takes me away from reality for a little bit. Time slips away and eventually Dylan comes into the room, and we get ready for bed without a word. He settles into a bottom bunk across the room, so I pull the lamp's string, and we are engulfed in darkness.

"Kat left you here," Dylan comments after a few moments.

"Sure did," I reply, not trusting myself to say more. It wouldn't be kind.

"And she probably didn't tell you how she ruined her chances at swimming professionally" he adds, but I don't answer. He fills in the gaps for me. "Well, constant tardiness and throwing team parties involving illicit drugs aren't part of keeping a good standing on any athletic team. At least they allow her to help coach."

"Kat never tells me anything like that."

"She's always drowning her feelings. Don't take it personal."

"Kinda hard not to."

He sighs and the bed creaks as he turns. "Yeah, you're right. You can't do much about a conceited person who doesn't want to change."

Finally, an answer to my uncertainties and questions about Kat. She's selfish. She wants me there when it's convenient for her or helpful: giving her answers to the math homework, setting up Taco Tuesdays, driving her and her friends to bars and frat parties, or to the mall when she wants retail therapy. *Our friendship is based on convenience. Right from the start,* I think, and the truth settles into my stomach like a heavy brick.

A light snore from Dylan's bunk tells me our conversation is over. But even this revelation doesn't excuse Kat's behavior to me. Which begs the question—why do I let her walk all over me?

Chapter 16

Thanksgiving And Festivities

I awake from a dream where I'm clawing at the air to stop my descent into an abyss. Heart pounding, I check my phone to find it's eight in the morning. My mind immediately turns to Kat. I take a deep breath.

I should be grateful I'm here.

Dylan lightly snores nearby. My bunk creaks when I move, but he doesn't stir. Grabbing my jacket and a book, I tiptoe toward the living room. The smell of bacon greets me as I pass the kitchen where Monica stands behind the kitchen island's built-in stovetop, spatula in hand and pancake batter bubbling in one gigantic frying pan while bacon cooks in a pan next to it.

"Good morning! Surprised to see you this early," Monica says as she flips pancakes then the bacon, the grease sizzling.

At least she's cooking real bacon and not the turkey bacon Mom makes.

I yawn, sitting on a cushioned chair on the other side

of the island. "I have morning classes, so I guess my body forgot how to sleep in."

"Good timing. The first batch of breakfast is done. There's fresh coffee in the pot too. Make yourself at home." She grabs a plate and piles a few pancakes and slices of bacon on it. She continues, "Listen. I'm sorry about last night. Dad means well, but he has expectations for his family that don't always...live up to modern times." She sets the butter dish, syrup, and silverware before me as well as the heaping plate of food.

I can work this off later somehow. They surely have a home gym here.

Drowning my plate in that maple-goodness, I say, "It's okay. All families have their issues."

She holds eye contact, her brown eyes soft and apologetic. "True. But it shouldn't be on full display when guests are over."

Between bites of food, I tread carefully with my next question. "If you don't mind me asking, how did the family business start?"

"Oh, I don't mind. It's a long story, but my great grandparents immigrated to the States and ended up in California. They farmed and grew vineyards, which turned into several wineries and a bustling farm, our family's livelihood.

When several droughts hit California, my parents moved to a quieter part of the country where they could farm and have a winery, if only a smaller one. But they remained involved with some of the business in California, so they were making money on both. Hence," Monica gestures to the room, "all of this. Successful farms, wineries, and wise investing brings us to the present."

"So, your dad doesn't like that Kat and Dylan aren't contributing to the family business?"

"They aren't the only ones. He picks on them for some reason. Probably because we live here with my parents. I've been employed by them my whole life. I wouldn't have been able to provide good things for Kat and Dylan on my own. But I don't expect my kids to follow in my footsteps."

This is the first mention of Kat and Dylan's absent father that I've heard.

She clears her throat. "Of course, my parents are only getting older, so when they bought this lake house, I moved in with Kat and Dylan to keep up the house, watch over my aging parents, and run the business. I make trips to our facilities here and in California."

"Sounds like a lot. My mom has her own marketing business, so I understand the dynamics."

"When you're working with family, it's hard to keep personal relationships untainted by business." She wipes her brow and peeks over her shoulder as voices sound from fellow early risers. "Well, it's Thanksgiving so let's try to enjoy today. Be thankful for what we have. As a warning, be prepared for lots of food and drinks. And talking." She returns her focus to cooking.

I devour the meal then clean my plate in the sink while Monica talks with the family members entering the kitchen, chatty and lively despite the hour. Filling a coffee cup, I sneak to the four-seasons porch to read. The words on the pages swim around, refusing to stick in my brain. I can't stop thinking about this family: their self-made, generational riches; a ruined professional swimming career; absent father and husband. What else is this family hiding?

Their life feels like it could be a novel.

I read paragraphs, stare out into the pines and daydream, and sip coffee until it jolts me awake. People venture into the kitchen, taking over cooking duties so Monica can eat. Dylan joins me, sitting next to me with his breakfast. We have polite conversation, nothing story worthy. Kat doesn't show up until noon. Her bloodshot eyes tell me she didn't sleep well or drank too much. Probably both.

The smells of cooking food fill the house: three roasting turkeys, baking bread, pies, mashed potatoes, even some homemade penne alla vodka; the noodles and sauce are made from scratch by an aunt. Monica recruits Dylan and I to set the tables with fine China dinnerware. Someone turns on the tv for the annual parade and football games. Conversation and laughter never cease. The family includes me in their discussions, but I can't remember most of their names and how they are related; my brain is preoccupied with the family drama.

I laugh, eat, drink and ignore my growing resentment of Kat.

Gorging on the delicious food and drinks takes us into the evening hours. Kat walks into the living room with her face smothered in makeup, hair pinned into a bun, and a purse clutched in her hands. Dylan and I acknowledge her while we lounge on the couch together.

She smirks at the sight of us. "Alright love birds. I'm off to shop until I drop or whatever. Don't miss me," Kat announces, then runs out the door to someone's car waiting in the driveway.

I open my mouth to answer, but she's already gone. Sighing, I glance over at Dylan. *Got an explanation for this time?*

He bites the inside of his cheek. "It's Black Friday. She and her friends have a tradition of going every year. There's a huge outlet mall a few miles up the road…" His voice trails off.

I take a long sip of the drink in my hand, the same red wine I had the night before.

Dylan swirls the wine in his own glass. "I'm sure she has a reason even if it's a dumb one."

You don't always have to defend her. I want to say this aloud, but I also don't want to start anything. Why voice my feelings on Thanksgiving to a man who refuses to commit to a relationship with me even if being here appears very relational to me?

That's a whole other issue I want to ignore too.

A family member turns on a classic Christmas movie, so I drop the subject and watch the cheesy movie, a welcome distraction. Dylan follows my lead and doesn't bring the topic back up. We laugh along with the family and drink our wine.

Kat isn't back by the time I go to bed.

~ ~ ~

Friday morning starts the same. Monica makes me over-easy eggs, toast, and freshly squeezed orange juice for breakfast, while we discuss school.

Monica leans over the sink, scrubbing at the dirty dishes. "Would you like to help me decorate for Christmas? No pressure of course since you're a guest. But I wanted to ask if that's something you enjoy."

"Sure! I loved decorating our house for Christmas," I say after a sip of the juice. I won't have time to set up decorations at home, and the dorm is too cramped. What if Dylan invites me back over for Christmas, and I can enjoy the festivities and decorations with everyone?

It will be a Christmas miracle, but a girl can hope, can't she?

Monica smiles and gestures toward one of the living rooms. "You're so sweet. Thank you. My brother brought up the boxes and tree last night after dinner. Here, I'll go with you."

Monica takes me past the dining room to the second living room–yes, the house has two of them–and I behold an artificial evergreen reaching to the ceiling.

Pointing to plastic boxes labeled 'ornaments', she says, "Why don't you start with the ornaments?" She grabs the tote labeled 'garland.' "Would you like me to put Christmas music over the speakers?" she asks as she balances the box on her hip. I nod and Monica disappears. A few moments later, soft piano music that I recognize as a Christmas hymn plays from the speakers throughout the room. Surround-sound Christmas music? I could get used to this.

Humming along to the familiar melody, I grab the box nearest to me. Inside are intricate circular glass ornaments. One by one, filling in the blank spaces, I hook them into the branches, the pristine hardwood floors warning me to be careful; don't want to be the person Dylan brings home who breaks nice things. I hang the ornaments as high as my arms will allow. Someone taller can do the rest of the tree.

One of the boxes is a shoe box rather than a plastic tote. Lifting the lid, I expose homemade ornaments, a contrast from the delicate bulbs that embellish the tree. Curiosity takes over as I sit and rummage through the keepsake Christmas crafts made by Kat and Dylan along with other ornaments from places they've traveled.

An ornament catches my attention: a hand-painted cardboard star with the name 'Mason' scribbled on it and a picture of a young boy with dark curly hair.

The boy named Mason is a copy of Dylan.

"Oh, I guess they brought up the personal ornaments," Monica says from the entryway. I jump, the box falling into my lap.

My heart pounds in my ears as I stand and step toward her. "Sorry. I was about to ask what you wanted to do with these." I put the lid on the box and extend it to her.

Monica takes it, holding it gingerly in her hands. "Not a problem. I usually put these on the tree in my bedroom." She looks down at the box, her eyes misty. Yet in a moment, it's over. Monica blinks and clears her throat.

"Thanks for helping. It's been years since Kat was interested."

She leaves, clutching the keepsakes, and I explore more boxes, noticing more specialized Christmas decorations with different initials, especially the letter M. I hold up a Christmas stocking that belonged to this Mason. I close my eyes, replaying conversations in my mind, wondering if I ever heard his name before.

Wait. The picture frame on Dylan's bedside table of him and Kat and another boy. My brain swirls with questions and hunches. Am I allowed to ask about him? Will I be crossing into territory that is not meant for me?

Trying to ignore my curiosity, I set up more decorations then return to read in the four seasons room. Dylan joins me with his breakfast. Mason's name almost spills out of my mouth multiple times, but I hold my tongue. Dylan has never mentioned him for a good reason, I'm sure.

The next few hours brim with continual holiday festivities: cooking, naps, card games, and watching movies, all of which are a distraction from me forming ideas about this mysterious Mason. Kat sticks around for some of it. Being here with Dylan feels normal and almost natural. It's as if we are dating, the way we interact and exist, but no strings tie us together.

What could I do to convince him otherwise?

Kat visits neighbors after dinner, insisting she's "doing us a favor by leaving us alone", so Dylan and I walk down to the massive dock in the backyard once the sun begins to set. Ripples of orange and pink twist in the sky before me, and it takes all my self-control not to jump into the water.

Dylan rummages through a bin and grabs out two fold-out camping chairs and blankets. I sit, pulling my knees up into the chair and wrapping one of the blankets around me. Dylan places his chair next to mine, fixing his gaze on the quiet lake free of boat-churned waters.

"I bet this place is fun in the summer," I comment after a few moments of silence.

Dylan shrugs, his eyes never leaving the water. "It was nice at first. Gets old though. It's been the same families here for years. Same people, same drama."

I turn to him. "Humans tend to ruin good things. But at least you have these opportunities to spend time with your family. It's been a long time since I've had something like this."

He nods. "You're right. As families go, we're close."

"Your mom is the sweetest thing." I clear my throat. "Can I ask—"

"About my dad," he answers as if he knows where my thoughts have lingered since I've been at the lake house. I guess his dad is a safer topic than Mason.

"No pressure. It's just hard not to wonder, hearing these family stories and talking with your mom every morning."

Dylan's fingers fidget with the blanket's edge. "He left when we were young. My grandparents helped my mom raise—" here his voices catches, but he recovers quickly and says, "—Kat and me."

So that's another reason Monica moved in with her parents—to have help with her two—maybe three—kids.

I place my hand over his. "I'm sorry."

He doesn't pull away from my comforting gesture but closes his eyes for a moment before replying. "It's okay.

Just sucks. I was three when he up and left."

"Have you heard from him?"

"Not a word. I tried to locate him once, but I think every kid does at some point."

I tuck my hand back under the blanket. Silence washes over the moment except for the water sloshing below us. One question remains about his family history. My chest tightens, knowing I'm about to cross an invisible line between Dylan and me, a deeper dive into his possible trauma. It could have consequences.

But I do it anyway.

"So, I was helping your mom put up Christmas decorations and I saw a few with someone named Mason on them."

Dylan stands, the chair almost toppling over. He points at me. "Don't go poking your nose into places it doesn't belong." He turns away from me. "I invited you here because you would be alone on a holiday. I felt bad. That's it." He storms off the dock, leaving me with the crisp air and descending dark night. I wrap my arms around myself, shame curling into my stomach. What did I expect from prying into his personal life? We aren't in a relationship. I don't have access to that part of his life unless he's willing to share it.

Obviously, he's not. And I don't blame him.

He's not such a bad guy, a little rough around the edges, but I cannot truly be with him. Here I am anticipating the day he slips away, the day when my delusion of us being more finally crumbles.

I remain on the dock until the nighttime chill convinces me to go inside. Deciding to ignore a few greetings from family members, I head to my room and take a long hot shower to avoid my feelings and thoughts as usual. I read until bedtime, but Dylan never returns to the room.

He avoids me most of Saturday, so I spend my last day here with Monica and various aunts and cousins; we bake cookies, play card games, and finish decorating. He returns to our shared bedroom that night, making small talk with me only.

I don't suspect I'll be coming back for Christmas, but I understand. I screwed this up big time. Yet again.

Chapter 17

Finals

The extended weekend with its festivities and spilled secrets inevitably ends. Kat insists she sit in the back seat for the ride back to school. I stare at the road ahead, and Dylan doesn't try to make conversation either. *Good job, Melanie.* I ruined whatever we had going for us. Dylan is supposed to be a distraction, but I'm wrapped up in his family history and drama.

Perhaps I have a thing for moody, unavailable guys?

Dylan keeps me around for unknown reasons. Either a true distraction or someone who will willingly return my affections—that's what I've been searching for. If he doesn't want anything more with me, what are we doing?

The entire ride back is quiet and inconsequential. Dylan takes Kat to her apartment then parks in front of my dorm. His hands grip the steering wheel, the lights from the dash lighting up his glum expression.

"I'm sorry, Mel," he says after a moment.

"What are you sorry for? I'm the one who asked."

"I shouldn't have brought you. I didn't want to send the wrong message, but I think I did."

Of course. Time to face the truth.

He bites his lower lip. "Listen. I have…baggage. I'm not ready to put that on someone again. I was dating that girl Lauren. She kept arguing with me about it. Wanting to get back together because I was being 'silly' and 'self-sabotaging'."

My face warms. "I'm trying to understand. You're sorry for bringing me to the lake house because that was a little more than casual?"

"Yeah. I was trying to be nice. Like a… friend."

I cringe. "I understand. I'm a good friend but not dating material." I tease, trying to make a joke about it. How else can I respond to this?

He sighs. "You're smart. You have places to go. I don't want to hold you back by this," he gestures to himself.

I don't want to argue with him; my nerves are fried from the tense car ride home. I grab my bag and force the car door open. "It's okay. I get it. You should go home. I need to get ready for classes tomorrow like the smart girl that I am."

He faces me with one of the grimmest expressions I have seen on him. Is it regret? Sadness? Worry, even? I'll never know. Before he can say another word, I step out and slam the car door, ignoring the gaping hole in the pit of my stomach. In that moment with my back turned, this marks the end of a possible relationship between us right now.

Back in my room I unpack my things, my body's movement automatic but numb like I'm on autopilot. It's not until I lay down that everything I've been pushing down erupts. Kat uses me, and Dylan is a lost cause. Their friends are theirs, not mine. I have two choices: keep doing the same things with the same results or find a new group of people to spend my time with.

Grabbing my phone, I click on text messages and scroll until I find Seth's contact. My finger hovers over his name. *Am I really doing this?* They'll include me if I make the first move. Seth has encouraged me multiple times to rush next semester. Why not get a start in making new friends?

I type to him: "Hey! Care if I join you at the bars this week?" Then I add to sweeten the deal on his end: "I could try weed too."

Within a few minutes Seth replies: "Finally got you. Yeah, first smoke is on me. But you have to come over and hang out with us."

Me: "Will do."

I'm on the verge of something new, and I don't know if it's a good thing, but I've made my choice.

~ ~ ~

Weeks fly by without time to process everything. Alcohol

makes it a blur. Weed, Molly, or whatever they offer me contributes to the madness and stress. Dylan is polite to me in class, not childishly avoiding me. His absence at the bars when I'm sober enough to notice is questionable. He doesn't text me to come over anymore.

I stopped letting Kat copy my math homework and setting up Taco Tuesday; I stopped hanging out at her place on Tuesdays altogether. We see each other in class and when we cross paths while out on Main Street, both of us are either drunk or high as kites.

Greek life doesn't make a fuss about me tagging along with them, smoking and drinking whatever, but that's the extent of my interactions with them—artificial and shallow.

Andre and Erin quit asking me to hang out, seemingly under the stress of finals. Erin doesn't speak when I pass her at the front desk; she only stares at her laptop. Andre mirrors this posture at work. I haven't seen them hanging out in the common rooms lately.

We're all drowning.

I'm no different except I'm tripping on caffeine, weed, and alcohol to keep my sanity. Perhaps they are contributing to the insanity, but I can't ignore the way most days pass through my fingers, and I can barely keep a grip on reality. I've never known stress like this. Why does it feel like the weight of the world is on my shoulders? Probably because whatever I do now will dictate my future. If I fail, the consequences are more detrimental than simply receiving a bad grade. My future depends on me not screwing up, which might be impossible for me.

Besides the accounting and Spanish finals, I sail through my other exams with A's. *Why was I so stressed?* Of course, I don't want to acknowledge that these are fundamental classes, and courses will only get harder from here.

That's what alcohol and weed are for.

On a freezing December morning, Kat and I leave the math classroom, our last final of the semester. Dylan sits on a bench outside of the building and joins us. The silence lies thick between us; Kat is preoccupied by something on her phone, while Dylan stares at the ground. What do I say after weeks of not speaking to them?

I'm bitter about everything.

Kat puts her arms around my shoulder and his as we walk side by side. She sighs, long and dramatic. "Well, we survived. It's time to par-tay. Where we going tonight?"

"I'm going home," Dylan says.

Kat crosses her arms. "We're free! Don't be such a downer."

He shrugs. "I'm tired. Want to be home for a little bit. Uninterrupted."

"Bro. You're hopeless lately. Can't get you to go out anywhere. What's your problem?" Kat stands in front of of him, blocking the way to his car. I stop and watch the scene unfold.

He throws his hands up. "You've decided not to care about your future. And everyone keeps telling me what I need to do about mine." Dylan takes a deep breath. "I need time to think without everyone being in my business. Especially you."

"Is *Nonno* pressuring you again to take over Mom's job so she can work less?" When Dylan doesn't answer, Kat sighs. "Well, don't take your indecision out on the rest of us."

He points at her. "You're one to talk." Dylan pushes past Kat to his car and drives away.

Kat swears and turns back to me. "He's been so dramatic lately. Guess I'll stay at the condo until Christmas. Anyway, you good for a little celebration?"

This is the first invitation out from her since Thanksgiving. I shake my head. "I haven't been home this semester, and it's a long drive."

"Ugh. Fine. Have a good Christmas!" She waves as she gets into her car.

"Yeah, you too," I call after her.

A boulder settles into the pit of my stomach. Finals are over. I survived my first semester of college. I can go home and relax for a few weeks. Then what's so wrong?

I don't let my mind dwell on it as I return to the dorm and pack one bag for three weeks at home and leave without another glance back. I'll return soon anyway.

Winter break drags out for six weeks, but I decided to take a writing class because I need another English credit. At least this is what I tell myself. The truth—what will I do at home for six weeks without classes and homework to fill my time?

The drive home is trivial, every road sign muddling into the darkening day. An hour away from Mom's house, snow dumps from the skies, and I grip the steering wheel with two hands the rest of the way home. I don't remember the drive which is good. My head is not a friendly place right now.

My car tires spin out in the fresh snow on the slightly inclined driveway, but I'm able to park in the two-car garage. Carrying my bag into the house, silence greets me. Mom must be working late. At least she has leftover soup in the fridge with the date she bought it written on its plastic lid.

I sit at the dinner table and text Hayley and Alex that I'll be home over the break. They instantly reply with confirmations, dates, and times they are available. This semester's communication has been mostly initiated by me, with the occasional mention of a funny occurrence from either of them. Much of the semester has been quiet between us. I should be thankful that they want to see me, right?

What's worse is I want to text Dylan or Kat, ask them how their mom is doing, and what their Christmas plans are. I can't sever friendships and connections. To hold off the pity party, I fall into bed and cocoon myself between fluffy blankets, a large stuffed monkey that Brady bought me, and my pillow. Sleep finds me as I watch snow collect on the windowsill.

If only I had a drink to numb these feelings.

~ ~ ~

"Remember that one time the literature professor…"

The lunch with Hayley and Alex consists of several instances of "Oh, you had to be there" and their simultaneous sips of milky brown mochas. I slurp a green smoothie as snowflakes float outside the window of the coffeehouse, the hangout of our high school years—years of reading books for hours, our notebooks spread across the table for tests we would ace every time.

Now I do this alone at college.

Hayley clears her throat, and I'm brought back to the present. She sits in front of me, the beige infinity scarf she crocheted wrapped snuggly around her neck. To her right, Alex crosses her arms over her high school track hoodie.

Hayley's high cheekbones raise as she grins. "So, Mel. There's this dude."

I wince at the nickname. This is not the time to think about Dylan.

"You are totally blushing. Details?" I ask.

She rolls her eyes. "He's an amateur actor working on getting into bigger shows. Wants to go to Broadway, as they do."

"So, you guys are…"

"Talking, but we have moved to good morning texts, so it's going in the right direction."

Alex snorts. "Lucky. I'm so single. Don't have time between the assistant coach gigs and school." She turns to me. "What about you? Seeing anyone?"

My head shakes with a definite no. "Nope. Me, myself, and I. Been really focusing on classes." It isn't a total lie. I omit details about occasional one-night stands, bar/frat house shenanigans, and that Dylan and I met because it's easier that way.

They nod in unison with pitiful smiles. "Sounds like high school. You were always so focused on your studies. Making the rest of us look bad," Hayley says.

"Yeah, Brady might have been smart in math, but you pulled him through his English and literature classes. How many hours did you tutor him and basically write his essays?" Alex asks.

Too much. I did too much for him. No use dredging up the past with them. I don't want their pity.

"Well, he's with someone new. He got what he wanted in the end," I conclude.

Hayley stares somewhere over my head and Alex cringes at my blunt but true statement. They don't bring him back up.

The rest of the lunch is more stories that I wasn't

present for. I stare into space while they chatter. There's no common ground between us anymore. What did we talk about in high school for four years? We are distinct human beings with history and no lasting bond, at least with me.

Why am I only realizing this now?

I sigh when I've had enough and stand up. "Well, I better get going before it starts snowing too much. You know how much I hate driving." I excuse myself from the table.

They rush through their goodbyes. "Bye, Mel. Merry Christmas." They give me quick side hugs then return to their conversation.

I turn my back thinking this might be the last time I see them. Well, that's probably too drastic. How do you continue friendships with people who share nothing but history with you? I have no emotional connection with them anymore; this whole afternoon felt like a masquerade, pretending to care about things I wasn't present for.

We are on different paths in life and that will have to be okay.

I shuffle my feet along the snowy ground to my car. The surrounding city hums and bustles, ceasing to rest. My eyes scan for something familiar, some comfort to make up for the past hour, but the city feels foreign. I grew up here, but it's not home anymore. I have no one to keep me here, and no reason except memories of people disappearing from my life like the snowflakes drifting in and out of my blurring vision. *Why cry now, Melanie? What's the point? They seem content without you.*

Why did I come back?

~ ~ ~

To be honest, Christmas Day is nothing spectacular anymore. The magic of the holidays ceased when my parents announced their separation a year ago. I went to Brady's house last year for Christmas to distract myself.

I cope so well with change.

The divorce is almost finalized. Things get ugly when one parent owns a business but both parents have shares in it and when one parent moves in with a new partner before the divorce is official; it also doesn't help that Mom is too busy.

Somedays I don't know who to trust. Who is telling the truth? I try to stay out of it as best as I can.

Christmas day begins at Mom's house with uncles, aunts, and cousins on her side coming and going, politely asking me about school and eating the meager lunch of store-bought rotisserie chicken and salad; before the split, Dad cooked a brisket every year. The morning and afternoon pass without excitement but also lacking any negativity other than Mom and the aunts complaining about this or that.

I read most of the day on the couch in the living room

to appear social.

Around dinnertime I drive to Dad's apartment through the snow-packed streets across town. Sharon, his girlfriend, welcomes me at the front door. She leads me into the apartment out of the falling snow and into the kitchen where a bottle of wine and three glasses sit on the counter. Dad rises from the couch to give me a hug.

"Merry Christmas, Mellie." He grabs a wine opener from a kitchen drawer. "I'll let you drink this. I figure you do at school anyway," he says as he pops the cork out and pours us each a glass. The maroon liquid warms my throat as I sip it.

"Thank you," I say as I sit at the little table in the dining room area connected to the kitchen.

"It was a gift from corporate for our good sales this year," Dad comments as he sets the almost empty bottle back on the counter.

Sharon giggles. "It's a gas station, not a sales job." She downs the wine in her glass. She'll be silly soon.

Dad shrugs. "I guess being a manager has its perks. They gave us a small end of year bonus too."

"Well, don't waste it on those Poker games you're always playing."

Dad rolls his eyes but doesn't defend himself. She often nags him about his Poker playing, television watching, or his less than glamorous gas station manager job. I have no idea what he sees in her, honestly.

I watch as he and Sharon prepare a dinner of steak and red potatoes in cast iron skillets. The food sizzles, filling the apartment with smoke and mouth-watering aromas. I close my eyes, my mind wandering away from the present to nowhere in particular, a blank space. In psychology they call it disassociating. I call it coping.

Dad clears his throat, and I open my eyes to see him staring at me. Sharon is gone.

"While she's in the bathroom, I wanted to ask you if you were okay. Not sure if your mom told you…" he begins.

"It's finalized, right? Mom didn't mention it."

He nods, his gaze shifting from me to the food.

I smile. "Well, good for you. You can move on. Officially."

The reason for their divorce is unknown to me; back to my 'who's story do I trust' point.

He avoids eye contact but replies, "Remember I have that guest room if you ever want to stay here. With your mom putting the house on the market, I'm sure it will be a wreck from packing."

"Thanks," I mutter as Sharon returns. Her humming tells me she's already tipsy. Must have been drinking before that one glass. Nothing new.

They finish prepping dinner while I take slow sips of wine, ignoring the weight of the finalized divorce and the unanswered questions surrounding it. Dad serves the food, our plates full of meat, potatoes, and pieces of sourdough bread.

Dad holds his glass up for a toast. "To new beginnings," he says and clinks his glass to my and Sharon's brimming glass.

They comment on the tasty food, but my mind wanders away from the present moment. One more week, and I'll be back at school. A new semester and opportunity for memories— the positive way to view it. I want to make the most of my time in college since I don't have another option.

There's a part of me that doesn't want to return. I don't belong anywhere. Kat and Dylan have disappeared, and my Greek life acquaintances don't try to get to know me; we get lit on booze or whatever but that's it. Then I wake up, work until I'm exhausted, study until I cry, and do it all over again the next day.

Why can't I make any positive changes in my life?

After dinner Dad hands me a wrapped present containing a beanie hat with the school's logo on it. I give him trouble for not always being present in my life, but at least he knows what I like.

I leave after watching a comical Christmas movie that Sharon ruins with her constant laughter. Mom is locked in her office when I come home, so I microwave a piece of apple pie one of my aunts brought today–Mom won't eat it–and head to my room.

Eating on my bed and staring into the snowy night, my own thoughts begin to swirl. I must make some kind of change. I can't continue this cycle, this wheel I try to run on that's getting out of control. Something needs to change, but what does that look like?

I hope I don't have a complete meltdown first.

Chapter 18

J-term

January 2015

Snow stalks me as I leave the dorm's warmth, footprint traces leading to the front of a looming brick building. Andre braves the cold next to me. The classroom within houses a chalkboard and an ancient rectangular heating unit that hisses and clanks—unwilling to modernize, rebelliously staying the same. Like me.

New year, same me.

This English course I'm taking during winter break focuses on creative nonfiction for non-English majors who need more class credits. It's the perfect excuse to get away from home and my dorm room; any model student would take a class during a break instead of recuperating from the semester, right?

The professor and head of the English department, Dr. Slate, leans against a podium as he surveys the class of ten students through his lensed, steady gaze.

He smiles, his eyes squinting. "You will need to pick

the topics for your final paper by Friday, so tomorrow. Remember, pick a group of people, a stereotype, or a culture, and write about it honestly and thoroughly. Tell me a new story that is true but creative. Tell me your truth, well, your perspective. Come up front if you need some advice. The rest of class is free writing time."

"Help me," I plead to Andre as other students file to the front to talk with Dr. Slate. Andre took the class for similar reasons: an excuse not to be stuck at home with his sisters. We didn't discuss taking the same course, but we rejoiced seeing a familiar face when walking to class the first day. It only lasts three weeks, but I would rather do this than sit at home, pack, and pretend everything is fine.

Andre holds up his hands. "I suggested you write about basic white girls."

I roll my eyes. "I'm not indulging that stereotype. Not sure if I fit that label anyway. I drink my coffee plain. What're you writing about?"

"Easy. About being a black man. But how do I tell it so people will listen but not feel like I'm telling them they're bad people?"

I place my hand on top of his for a moment, hoping he takes it as a friendly gesture. "You're an inspiration. I mean that."

His smile widens, and he sits up straighter than he already has been. "Thank you, CEO Melanie. Trying my best." He pretends to contemplate something. "Well, you could write about being the heiress of an illustrious marketing firm and how the pressures of nepotism are a burden…" His voice trails off, perhaps waiting for a laugh.

My shoulders drop a little. "Yeah, it's a heavy burden, for sure."

The day after Christmas Mom started packing up the house, a 'For Sale' sign lodged in the front lawn of the home I grew up in. With the divorce finalized, she would have to downsize and move into an apartment. Saying goodbye to my childhood home was more emotional than I expected. I left for college on New Year's Day in tears, memories flooding my mind the entire six-hour drive back here.

Andre interrupts my reminiscing. "I'm going to talk to Dr. Slate about my paper. You'll find a topic to talk about, I'm sure of it. From glancing over at your work a few times, you're a great writer too."

I cover my face to hide a small blush as he walks over to our professor, leaving me to wonder about my story topic. The minutes tick away, but I'm no closer to an idea.

"Are you all right, Melanie?" Dr. Slate asks as he packs his leather satchel.

I glance around to discover I'm the only student in the classroom. Shrugging, I tell him, "I'm having trouble deciding on a topic. Might be taking it too seriously."

He chuckles. "I've had you in class for almost two weeks now, so I can assure you that you're thinking too hard about it."

"I want it to be the right topic."

"Pick something you know. A snapshot of it. The closer it is to you, the better you'll write it. Once you can tell your story, then you can tell others' stories."

I don't want to tell my "story". I'm trying to avoid it.

I mutter, "Thanks, Dr. Slate. I'll see you tomorrow morning with a topic."

~ ~ ~

Andre texts me later that afternoon, asking if I want to work on our assignments in the lounge that evening. I accept, and after dinner we sit together in the first-floor lounge, our laptops resting on the long table and a bowl of popcorn between us. I thought being here with him would help me focus on my paper. He's typing away while I stare at a blank screen.

My phone buzzes back-to-back, a welcome distraction from my writer's block. Dylan's name flashes across the top of two consecutive text messages.

The first text is simple: "Hey, Mel. It's Dylan." The next one reads: "Of course, you know that. Want to meet up later tonight?"

Really, Dylan?

He wants me to come over and act as if everything is okay between us. I sigh and drop my phone on the table without replying.

Andre stops typing. "You good?"

I pause, debating whether to tell him the truth or not.

He notices my hesitation. "It's alright if you don't want to tell me. We don't talk about personal things often."

"Just a situation with a guy." I lean back slightly in my chair, frowning at the ceiling.

"Well, he can wait. We have to find a topic for your paper."

Without hesitation I say, "Hookup culture."

Andre's eyes widen. "Oh, dang. I wasn't ready for that. You sure?"

"I mean. Dr. Slate told us to write about what we know." Where is this honesty coming from? I'm way too upfront with him about this.

"What would you write about specifically?" He grabs a handful of popcorn, his gaze thoughtful.

Why isn't he taken aback by my brash idea? Something about Andre and his sincerity makes me feel safe enough to keep talking.

I cross my arms, letting my thoughts spill out, unfiltered. "It's like, we're scared of commitment, but sometimes we want it. So, we settle for a distraction. Hooking up feels safer and easier than commitment." I glance down at my phone with its unreturned messages from Dylan and continue. "It only makes the problem worse. Feelings come along sometimes. And you get let down because it was only supposed to be casual until it wasn't for one person."

Now I've dumped part of my personal life onto Andre. I risk a glance, but he's stroking his chin, taking in what I said.

He turns to me, his eyebrows drawn together as he sets a hand on my shoulder and gives it a light squeeze. "Thanks for trusting me with that hurt." He doesn't break eye contact. "Sometimes culture makes the things it promotes appear glamorous and harmless. But society doesn't always want to admit the consequences of things like hookup culture."

Rubbing my temples I mutter, "I'm sorry. I didn't mean to drop that on you at once."

"You don't have to apologize. I asked." He gives me a knowing look. "You're not going to write about that, are you?"

I shake my head. "No. I'll probably pick something...safer."

He shifts, facing his laptop. "Sometimes the boat needs to be rocked, and people need to hear the truth no matter how uncomfortable. But it's not time for that yet. You're not ready, are you?"

I don't answer, so he fills the silence. "Well, some friendly but unsolicited advice. Take it or leave it but don't keep seeing that guy. You deserve better."

"Thanks for listening, Andre."

"Anytime."

The final project and reading of said project to classmates is due next Friday. I have to decide on a topic by class tomorrow, something that won't cause a stir or make my peers roll their eyes and scoff. There's no reason to speak up if no one agrees with me, right?

Well, except Andre.

I'm overcomplicating things. My life is a simple to-do list: give this final presentation, start my new classes, rush for a sorority, and make friends. New beginnings as my dad said. This is my chance to start over at university.

Any sound advice from Dad and Andre doesn't influence my next decision. All self-control slips as I text Dylan that tomorrow would be better for me to hang out. We agree to meet up for dinner.

Guilt settles in my stomach. *What a hypocrite.* Here I am telling Andre that hooking up has consequences, but I don't change my ways. I fall back into the same routine, wondering what it will take to break this vicious cycle.

~ ~ ~

On Friday evening, Dylan and I casually eat grilled chicken and fries at the dining hall. We comment on the food, but not much else is said. Sophia is at home, so we end up back in my room and underneath the bed sheets as if nothing has changed.

Afterward, Dylan and I lay side by side but not touching. He fiddles with the fringe on the fleece blanket covering us but doesn't say anything.

I break the silence. "You never mentioned winter break. I bet the lake house was beautiful on Christmas."

"Yeah. Christmas was good. But I don't want to talk about it."

"Why?"

His eyes remain on the ceiling. "Because I don't want to talk about my life or family."

I sit up, towering over him for once. "Then what are we doing? There are plenty of people around campus you can mess around with."

He sits up too, eye to eye with me. "I thought this was consensual."

"Sure. At one point. Tell me, am I just too nice or too willing?"

"What do you want, Mel? You told me you were okay with this."

"Things were fine until you started playing boyfriend, ghosted me, then reappeared like my knight in shining armor for another round. What am I supposed to think?"

He shakes his head, jaw clenched. Unmovable. Nothing I say gets through to him. Now I know how Lauren must have felt dealing with his stubbornness.

I spring from the bed, the anger finally seeping out. "You're a terrible person or whatever you want me to believe you are. You're just like Kat. You happy now?"

"No...no, I'm not happy. But here you are anyway."

Suddenly, I'm aware I'm not covered by the blankets

anymore. I snatch a robe from the floor and wrap it around myself. But I'm not done yet. I grip the bed, my knuckles white on the purple sheets.

"So, this is my fault? Because everything has been super casual. Every person hooking up meets the other person's family and hears all about their trauma."

It's been said before. We'll have the same argument, but it won't be resolved. We want different things.

He throws the blanket and sheets back, climbing out of the bed. I turn my head away, my limbs heavy and cold as he puts his clothes on.

Somehow, I find the courage to say to his back, "From the start I wanted us to be something more, and this isn't what I had in mind."

Dylan pauses at the door, his hand holding it ajar. Right when I think he's about to leave, he says no louder than a whisper, "Mason. He was my twin brother."

His use of past tense puts me in my place. In an instant my anger evaporates. I step closer to him, my heart dropping to the floor. *Why is he telling me this?*

The door shuts, but he still faces it. "We went to a high school party, we got drunk, and he drove us home. I survived. He—" Dylan's voice cracks.

"Why are you…" I begin, but I can't find my words either.

He turns to me but won't look me in the eyes. "I brought you home. Of course, you would find out about

222

him eventually. You should know the reason you can't be with me." He pauses. "And you're right. I've used you as a distraction from many things. I'm no better than Kat."

The rest of the puzzle pieces fall into place: why Dylan drinks but never gets drunk enough for any consequences; why he always drives his teammates home; why he doesn't try anymore even though he's more than capable; why he won't date me or anyone.

He has survivor's guilt. Badly.

"Dylan, you can't blame yourself forever. You have to keep living for…Mason's sake. You're smart and—"

"Would a smart person let a drunk teenager drive?"

The sentence hangs heavy between us. We trap each other in a stare before he spins back toward the door and leaves without another word.

I stand, stiff and unthinking, for some time until my body tells me it's unnatural. Burrowing back under the sheets, I curl into myself. No tears fall, but a desensitized sensation comes over me. It's a numbness I can't find a metaphor to describe. My head is empty of anything though I'm not inebriated. I lay in bed wrapped in my robe until I can't remember the difference between being awake and asleep.

I don't dream at all.

Chapter 19

Spring Semester

"Sex is only physical, and we buy that lie because it's easy to believe when you want commitment but are too afraid of it."

I prattle on about hookup culture to a room full of my peers enthralled by my bold statements. Applause fills the classroom once I finish, and I mock bow for my final presentation.

At least in my head, that's how it concludes.

I decided my topic by last Friday's deadline: the stereotypes of high school theater kids because it's safe, fun, and ignores my conflicted feelings about Dylan. At least the reading of my paper got a few chuckles and grins from everyone.

Other students present their final papers, but I don't pay attention until it's Andre's turn; he waits until he is the last person. Andre strides to the podium in his wrinkle-free button-down shirt and tie. Standing confidently, he narrates his paper, his words and delivery moving the class as we take in his perspective on being a black man. I am too wrapped up in his narrative, in trying to understand his perspective, to capture his speech word for word.

He concludes, and claps erupt from our small group. Without his prompting, we break into discussion about race from our surprisingly diverse class. I don't leave this conversation ashamed of my skin color, but rather, with more understanding and compassion for people who look different than me but are still like me in more ways than people want to focus on. Rather than arguments that go nowhere, the classroom is full of empathy and understanding.

The discussion dies down, so Andre takes a seat. Dr. Slate replaces him at the podium.

Our professor's contemplative eyes survey the room. "Thank you, Andre for your perspective and that important follow-up discussion. And to everyone else for sharing your stories and lives. I believe you gained something from this class. If anything, I hope you're more inspired to change the world around you for the better of everyone." He continues after adjusting his glasses. "I will post your grades as soon as I'm able. Thank you for a great class. Keep writing and telling your story."

Everyone packs their bags and leaves, but Dr. Slate approaches Andre and me.

He grins. "Honestly, I read your papers first. You had exceptionally written narratives. Have either of you considered English as a major or minor?" he asks.

Andre shrugs. "I'm too busy with political science, unfortunately. But this class was good for me. It got people thinking too."

Dr. Slate turns to me for my answer.

I want to major in journalism.

I stiffen. Where did that come from?

I avoid his gaze. "I'm in business. Not sure how I could add that to my schedule."

Dr. Slate sighs in defeat. "I understand. At least I tried. Well, I have office hours if you ever need help with an essay. My door is always open."

We thank him then Andre and I step outside into the cold, the Midwest winter unforgiving. I shove my gloved hands deeper into my coat pockets.

"We are free at last! Erin and I are getting dinner tonight. You in?" Andre asks.

"I'll let you know. I'm not feeling too well," I automatically reply. I mean, it's not a hundred percent false, but I don't want to socialize today or most days lately.

It's not them. It's me. Always me.

"We'll hang out when you are up to it," he says.

We split ways at the dorm's entrance. My mind starts spinning as I ascend the stairs. What I didn't say is I'm stressed. Permanently. J-term is over which means second semester will commence in a few days. How will I handle another semester of two jobs, homework, rebuilding a social life, and ignoring the pressures from Mom about my future?

And the fact I didn't get into the freshman honor's society because of my grades like she wanted.

I crawl into bed and notice a piece of paper on my nightstand. It's my second semester schedule that I printed with classroom locations and times:

-Microeconomics *(What does the 'micro' mean?)*

-College Algebra *(I'm not emotionally ready for this.)*

-Accounting II *(I passed Accounting I with a C.)*

-Business Management *(We'll see if I can manage a business.)*

-World History *(Should be an easy A.)*

-Nutrition *(For a science credit.)*

Then I'll be at admissions followed by the retail store. Somewhere before, between, and after that I'll do homework, join a sorority, and forget everything for a few hours at bars, clubs, and frat parties.

I did it once. I'll have to survive again.

The longer I lay there, ignoring my growling stomach, my thoughts wander. Especially after talking to Monica about her family and the business, I want to switch my major. Nothing major, right? I appreciate Mom's vote of confidence, but I have no idea how to run a successful business. Nor do I want to right now.

Why am I pursuing a business major then? To please my mom? To appear successful in everyone's eyes? To make more money? I don't know what I'm doing anymore.

Trying to ignore the tears threatening to spill over, I snatch my phone to text Kat of all people. She was rude during Thanksgiving and stopped inviting me out, but I can give her a second chance. I was being dramatic anyway.

I text Kat: "Hey! How was your winter break?"

An hour passes. She replies: "Great. Slept in so much. You?"

I immediately answer: "Break was boring, but I took a fun class. Writing. Loved it."

Kat: "Haha. Nerd."

Dead end conversation. There's no follow-up text.

Me: "Whatever haha. When are you getting back to campus? We need to hang out and drink."

She doesn't reply for another thirty minutes.

Kat: "Forgot to tell you I'm not coming back."

My heart pounds as my fingers press the words: "What do you mean?"

Kat: "I'm not coming back to campus."

Me: "Why?"

Kat: "School isn't my thing.

Me: "Let's hang out soon. I know where you live."

Kat: "K."

I can't breathe. Panic pushes against my chest, threatening to erupt. It's not only her. It's everything. Together, compounded. The move and life transitions. Brady. Classes and grades. Work. My future depending on my present decisions. Dylan. Now Kat.

This is the last time I'll talk to Kat because that's how our "friendship" works; no strings attached. Part of my brain assures me she isn't much of a friend. We party. We drink and gossip, but she knows nothing about me, nor has she asked. No connection, no comradery.

She was the first person to reach out to me and take me under her wing. I was grateful at the time, but in the end it is shallow. The two of us wading through liquor and drugs, upper and downers all night long only to do it again and again.

I'm alone. Truly.

And the panic swallows me whole.

~ ~ ~

Monday morning and a new semester dawn in low drab clouds with a chill crashing through me harsher than usual. I shuffle through the snow to my first class of the day, Microeconomics, all the while letting my thoughts take me wherever. Naturally, my mind goes to the people in my life.

Well, the ones now missing.

Dylan hasn't texted me since our glorious falling out.

Only noncommittal messages from Kat about drinking sometime this week. I'll have to let them go.

But I'm going to be sad about it first.

I miss talking to Erin in the mornings; even though, come to think of it, I hadn't seen her in the morning for months. Did she stop attending her morning class last semester? I've been so caught up in my own stuff I didn't think to ask what happened. She's always buried under books and homework when she works at the front desk. I'd hate to bug her.

Every time I see Andre, guilt lodges in my throat— guilt that I couldn't be bold about hookup culture as he was when he told the class about the racism and prejudice he has experienced; how I went back to Dylan after I condemned our habits; how some messed up part of me misses Dylan and wants him back.

My first class of the new semester resides in the bustling business hall; the room isn't hard to find. I spot lacrosse hoodies across the room, but thankfully it's Isaac and Ben. Isaac makes eye contact with me and waves me over. My heart rate picks up as I join them. *Has Dylan said anything about me?*

I greet them as I sit next to Isaac with Ben on the other side of him.

"Thanks to you we passed Spanish. We should give you an honorary seat at our games in the spring," Isaac says, a wide grin across his face. His brilliant smile doesn't keep me from noticing the dark circles under his eyes. He probably pulls some all-nighters like the rest of us.

A blush creeps across my face. "Dylan and I—"

Isaac interrupts, "You don't have to explain. Dylan has been a little…off lately."

"It's a lot of pressure when you have to pick a major but aren't sure what to do," Ben adds.

True, Dylan is a sophomore. He'll have to declare a major sooner than later. *Will he stay in the family business like me? Darn. He'll be in my classes if he does.*

I'm unsure what to say, but the professor trudges into the room, saving me from the rest of the conversation. The professor starts teaching right away after going over the syllabus and assigns us homework due Wednesday.

The semester is off to a great start.

My next class, College Algebra, is the same as the last one. Jessica and Dani are in this class with me, but they are surrounded by sorority sisters and teammates, so I opt not to speak or sit by them; what can I say or do to make them interested in me, anyway?

I'm leaving algebra when someone yells my name. I turn to find Seth and an instant but fake smile springs to my face. I must keep the Greek life people impressed, so they'll accept me when I rush soon.

"Long time no see. How are you?" I ask.

Seth places an arm over my shoulders. "Break was great. I did absolutely nothing but chill and smoke.

Anyway, rush week is next week." He hands me a flier. "One of the sorority girls told me to give this to anyone interested. This is the general meeting, but you'll do that chick stuff and find the right house for you or whatever."

"Are you doing anything tonight?" I ask.

"Main Street at 8. It's been a while. You need a ride?"

"I'll drive myself. Tell me where you're at when you get too Main."

That night I sit by myself at a bar for a while because 8 p.m. means 9 p.m. to others. But soon enough, the night is roaring in my ears, and I chain myself to the night's chaotic rhythm. I hop from bar to club and back again with a sullen Harrison, a rowdy Seth, and whoever else they drag along with them. The night's tempo never changes: the ceaseless drinks, the meaningless dancing and grinding, weed for the calm, and Molly for the high. The highs keep us from our own low, that is, until morning brings reality back. We stay running from it, whatever that is to each of us.

On Saturday morning, I wake up at their frat house with some random guy; I play right into the hands of our modern colleges' stereotype. I'm the poster child. Then I'm alone until the next night out, the next party I beg to join. I'm the fun-loving, giggling freshman swirling around everyone, high as a kite, light as a feather. I tell everyone that life is great.

Isn't it? No, I can't even fool myself.

I'm afraid of the lows, so I found some artificial highs. But when does this end? What will wake me up? This isn't healthy. Sure, it's normalized, but I'm slowly finding out that doesn't make it a good idea. Why do I keep participating in the madness, chained to the rhythm of a frantic dance I question but never quit?

When will I find enough courage to change?

Chapter 20

End of January

My typical Friday night begins at a bar. Harrison, Seth, and I lean against the wall, a double shot finding its way down our throats. That's when Lauren and a squad of sorority girls approach. Harrison stands up straighter. Seth mimics him while his wandering eyes drink in their exposed skin. I shrink, hiding in the shadows.

Lauren is practically glowing, beaming with her pearly white teeth. "Seth, nice to see you've joined a frat. And Harrison, it's been a while since we've talked. How are you?"

Harrison leans closer to her, confident despite his alcoholic tendencies. "Junior year is great. Have my internship lined up with a solid financial firm."

She laughs. "Oh my gosh! Congrats. You'll be an actual adult. I—"

"Hey, can I buy you a drink?" Harrison interrupts.

Lauren's smile never falters even as she follows him to the bar. Harrison buys them each a shot and within seconds, the liquor disappears.

It's not long before we're all on the dance floor, Lauren and Harrison facing each other but not touching. Seth is somewhere behind me pressing in closer. I playfully push him away, but he doesn't budge. I escape to the bathroom but rejoin the crowd eventually. Everything is fine; the drinks and laughs unceasing.

It's alcoholic-saturated bull crap.

Music presses against us, pulsing and pushing us into a wave of human bodies. Lauren and Harrison sway merely inches from each other. Something in my brain is telling me to separate them. Lauren is dating Isaac. I see them around campus and parties together, always whispering and smiling.

I stumble toward Lauren and Harrison but never make it to them. Bodies crush me as people step on my feet, impeding my mission. I say something–at least I think I do–but my words drown in the bar's unceasing cacophony.

Jessica appears and puts herself between the two and all is well in the world before anything gets too serious. Why couldn't I do that? Oh yeah, I'm too messed up on liquor.

Seth dances close to me, hands exploring. I swat him away, and he takes the hint. He's elsewhere now, so I lean against the wall, safe from the ebb and flow of bodies. The world sways before me, a persistent dizziness that won't leave me alone. A vice grip clutches my stomach, leaving me nauseous. *I need to sober up.*

An hour or so later, someone drives Seth, Harrison, and me back to a random fraternity house. The house vibrates with music and shouting even though it's almost midnight. Through the twisting smoke and dim lights, I find a corner to hide away while the party rages around me. *I need to sober up.*

My bladder complains that it might burst. I push past the crowds and search the house for a bathroom.

Seth stumbles into the hallway, nearly knocking me over. "Look who I found. What cha doin'?"

"Trying to find a bathroom," I answer, leaning away from his cigarette-saturated breath.

"I got you." He fiddles with every bedroom doorknob until one door opens, and he leads me into the room.

I break free minutes later, stumbling out of the bedroom into the hallway. His vile words at my back and the pulsing music swallow up the cry forming on my lips. No one speaks to me as I escape into the cutting January night air. Just another partygoer with heels clutched in trembling hands and horrors bigger than any human ought to carry hanging from their shoulders.

~ ~ ~

Sunday afternoon finds me cocooned in blankets that I haven't left except to use the bathroom and eat microwavable meals. My fingers freeze above my phone, a disturbing article staring up at me. The news headline informs readers of a recent case of an assaulted young woman. In the article, they call the victim a "Doe," but her perpetrator's name controls the television headlines and news articles with the unraveling story:

A California woman in her early twenties went to a fraternity party on January 18th, 2015, and wound-up unconscious from intoxication. While leaving she fell victim to assault. The perpetrator is a freshman who was drunk, and claims he gave in to peer pressure, drinking, and promiscuity. He blames the environment and his peers.

The details are alarmingly typical but not lost on anyone. In the following weeks, people will speak up about it, spreading awareness across college campuses and bringing this dark deed to light. That is, until the next story takes its place, and she is forgotten.

It happens every time.

We see ourselves in this Jane Doe: afraid to walk alone; afraid of tampered drinks; afraid of wearing a shirt a little too low or a skirt a little too high; afraid of saying no but not being listened to. We see her, and we see ourselves. And we are terrified.

I—I am terrified.

Reading the article's contents emanates cascading waves of anxiety throughout my body. The shaking starts, and I drop my phone, the article disappearing from my sight but not my mind. The panic attack follows soon after. These episodes have been happening the last two days. I breathe in and out, in and out until I remember where I am—safe in my room and away from the world.

I'll have to return to my normal schedule soon, but I can't ignore the terror buzzing underneath my skin, ready to burst and swallow me whole at any moment. The truth sinks in. I am Jane Doe. Another victim. And no one knows but me.

Who would I tell anyway?

~ ~ ~

I manage to get a few days off from classes, telling my professors I'm sick. I can only miss so many days; I will have to face my peers and the possibility of running into him.

When I return to classes I keep my head down, talk to no one, and focus on my classes and work. Microeconomics. College Algebra. Accounting II. Business management. World history. Nutrition. Admissions for a few hours then the retail store. Homework. Sleep. Repeat.

I see him as I walk to classes, but the buffer of students keeps panic from manifesting in public; it stays curled in my stomach, waiting for an unexpected moment to rear its head. He hasn't texted or approached me. I watch him go about his life, interacting with the other Greek life members as if nothing is wrong. As if nothing happened. He gets to enjoy his nights without consequences.

He gets to forget and move on.

But for me, there are no more parties. No nights at bars or clubs. I can't go out. I don't trust anyone. The most reliable and consistent thing about my day is when I climb into my dorm bed after each day is done. Alone.

Harrison has messaged me, but I ignore his texts. I never want to see him or any of his frat brothers again. Why bother joining a sorority? It will be impossible to avoid the fraternities the way Greek life intermingles.

I'm inconsequential. Drowning. I know the cliche is to keep moving forward. I tell myself that every day like a mantra, an anchor to positivity. But my feelings haven't changed.

The days blur together.

Sitting at my desk one February evening, the numbers and formulas in my textbook won't stick to the page or to the part of my brain that understands anything. I shove the book and homework, and they meet the floor with a *thud*. I slump at my desk, dragging my hands down my face.

There's a slight knock on the closed bathroom door followed by a muffled, "Are you okay?"

I open the door to find Erin. I almost ask her the same thing. Her eyes are puffy as if she hasn't slept in days, and her skin is sickly pale. I haven't seen much of her lately.

I fumble with my words. "Yeah. Sorry. I dropped my

book."

She yawns. "That's okay. Wanted to make sure no one was hurt."

"Haven't seen you lately. You studying too much like me?" Code for 'Are you drowning too?'

Erin's eyes don't meet mine. "Yeah. Um, lots going on. I should be getting back to it." Code for 'I don't want to talk about it.'

"Goodnight, Erin," I say before the door shuts.

I pick up the book from the floor and crawl into bed. *Tomorrow will be different*, I promise myself.

Microeconomics. College Algebra. Accounting II. Business management. World history. Nutrition. Admissions for a few hours then the retail store. Homework. Sleep. Repeat. The monotony is not only comforting but also frightening somehow.

Maybe tomorrow will be better.

Chapter 21

Spring Break &
The Following Unimportant Weeks

Sitting on the guest bed of my dad's apartment, I read every social media post from my peers at the beach. The notorious Spring Break trip: the beach, booze, and memories made but never remembered. I'm envious of their fun regardless of my choice to be sober.

Instead of partying I hold an icepack to my swollen face.

Spring Break 2015 started last Friday when I went home and had my wisdom teeth removed. Mom sold the house and is unpacking her two-bedroom apartment, so Dad took off a few days from work to help me. After dry heaving out of his truck's door on the way home from the surgery, we learned I can't handle anesthesia or an entire painkiller; the result is the same as the days I used to drink too much and found myself near a toilet.

I've been sitting in front of the TV eating coconut ice cream and soup since my surgery. My school routine has been replaced by another mindless regimen. I should go outside for fresh air and sunshine.

Another movie wouldn't be so bad, would it?

The movie will distract me from the jealousy and melancholy that I can't let go of. Hayley and Alex went to the beach for Spring Break; they didn't ask me to come along, even before the surgery was planned. I haven't hung out with anyone else at school, and no one has reached out to me. I've become invisible.

What's the point of trying anymore if nothing changes?

I don't want to go back to school or stay in this bed. Part of me sees nothing wrong with getting in my car and driving nowhere. Plant roots in a random town and start over.

If I don't have enough courage to do that at university, what makes me think I could start over elsewhere?

~ ~ ~

I return to school regardless of my somberness. On Monday morning, I stare at the microeconomics gibberish on the screen before the lecture begins. Besides this class, College Algebra, and Accounting II, my grades are decent this semester. My brain refuses to understand these simple concepts. The school's tutoring center is the only thing keeping my College Algebra grade from literal failure.

A random student walks past me, and I catch a whiff

of his cologne. My stomach drops and air catches in my throat.

I can't breathe.

I try to exhale. *Don't cause a scene. Breathe through it.* Tears swell, and my lungs forget their job. I flee the classroom, barely remembering to grab my books and bag. The world sways while my heart pounds in my ears. Collapsing into the stall of the nearest bathroom, my stomach caves in on itself while sweat beads on my forehead. The only sound I hear is my breath, rapid and unnatural.

The hysteria passes, and two details stick out in my mind. A smell alone triggered panic, and no one asked if I was all right; no onlookers or anyone in the bathroom.

I've disappeared.

If no one sees me and I'm alone now, what's the point of anything?

~ ~ ~

Friday night finds me sprawled on my bed with drooping eyes, the overtime at work taking its toll on my body. I'm permanently exhausted, burning out. Tired is too weak of a word. Frantic? Frenzied? The school bill must be paid regardless of how I feel.

My stomach growls. I should eat more. Dinners are easy to skip these days with working so much. Instead, I scroll through social media watching everyone pre-game and get ready to go out for the night. I should unfollow these people; they aren't my friends anymore. I watch them from afar as they live on, completely unaware of me.

Party Melanie gets people's attention. Party Melanie is calm and confident. She knows what to say, how to flirt, and charm anyone. Everyone likes Party Melanie. She is invited out. I wish I could be her all the time.

I sit up in bed, having a light bulb moment like some cartoon character. I saved a few bottles from my nineteenth birthday last fall. Upon learning it was my birthday, Kat dragged me to the gas station by her condo and bought me a bottle of flavored vodka and a handful of shots while I waited outside. Instead of drinking the bottle and doing shots that night, I hid them in my room.

No alcoholic drink has passed my lips since January, but I don't think twice about it as I pull out the first shot glass and the full bottle of flavored vodka. I turn on the show I'm currently binge-watching. The first shot goes down with a cough afterwards then I twist open the vodka. I'll be able to be Party Melanie without the loud noises and people shoving me around.

I don't stop drinking, even when the thoughts turn sour rather than sweet.

I'm like everyone else with problems. Why woe is me? Dumb Melanie. Why did I think I could make friends here? No one even likes me. Why did I think I could have a career I enjoy? Nothing ever changes. Stupid Melanie with her stupid dreams and stupid habits.

I'm the problem. Everyone leaves me. How could it be anyone's fault but my own?

The vodka and shot bottles slowly disappear. That next sip, that's my world. Burning my insides on the way down, an inferno sets in my veins. Repeat. Repeat. Repeat. Me, myself, and I.

And this drink.

A sinking sensation overcomes me, pushing me down on my bed. Heavy and warm. Shrinking into nothingness. Swirling. Floating. A gray haziness settles over my eyes. Tunnel-vision. I'm stuck on a train heading nowhere fast.

Am I finally free of this place?

No.

I want to be free.

What is that light? Yes, a car headlight. Why is there a car in my room?

A chill envelopes me. Wait. This isn't right. I wanted to be happy. Help me warm up. Where am I? I can't move my body. Please. Someone. Is anyone there? Can anyone hear me?

"Melanie. Are you okay?"

Is something wrong? Yes. I can't see or move. But who is talking?

"Melanie! Please wake up!"

I can't. It's empty and dark. Where am I? Help me.

Chapter 22

Sometime, Somewhere

I'm breathing through what feels like a straw. Mechanical exhalations. Cords clutch me, entangling my hand. Some part of me is aware of my surroundings, but my brain is reeling, only picking up on my immediate senses; I'm freezing, and my head and stomach are twisting into themselves. There's movement around me, but I keep my eyes closed.

I'm lying in a hospital bed.

The emotions hit me next: shame and fear relentlessly writhe in my gut. I could have died. I know what they did to me too—pump my stomach while these IVs replace the important things I've lost.

I've lost so many important things.

Sometime later, between nurses coming in and out, I open my eyes, but no one is here with me. Who did I expect to find? Someone called 911 and saved me from myself. I'll find out soon enough.

A nurse refills my IV and begins removing the tube

snaking into my mouth. I cough, fearing vomit, but nothing happens. Perhaps alcohol has done its damage, and I'm left with the consequences of pain and depleted self-esteem.

My mind wanders as I stare out the room's only window. What did I expect? What did I think I would find chasing after people who, in the end, don't care about me? What did I expect if I tried to get perfect grades, work myself to the bone, and accept any person who offered a semblance of friendship or romance? What did I think would happen if I drank myself into darkness?

The nurse hands me my phone, interrupting my thoughts. No new messages are waiting on the screen; it tells me it's noon on Saturday. Unsure who to contact, I text my mom, explaining where I am without telling her the cause.

A moment after it's sent, my cellphone rings. "Are you okay?" she asks. The concern in her voice evident.

"Yeah. They are releasing me soon."

"Okay. Well, have them send me the bill. I'll take care of it."

I can't complain, only bewildered by her kindness. Her lack of asking the reason for me needing the procedure is questionable. Does she think stomach pumping is a common thing for college students?

"Thanks," I manage to say before she hangs up.

I don't text Dad because I don't want to worry him.

He'll hear all about it this summer when I stay over there, when I'm less embarrassed to talk about it.

Within the hour, I'm discharged with instructions to eat light meals, drink plenty of water, and a subtle but stern comment about staying away from alcohol.

Don't have to tell me twice.

I take a cab back to the dorm, finding a hand-written note at the edge of my bed. I obey its instructions and knock on the Resident Director's door. I've seen Nikki around the dorm before, but all Kat and Harrison said of her is that she's religious and judgmental. *Just like those hypocrites in high school. Great. Here we go.* I swallow, my mouth dry. I imagine Nikki's upturned nose and frown as she gives punishment to a stupid freshman getting caught drinking in their dorm room.

The door swings open and standing before me is Nikki wearing an artsy apron, a paintbrush in her hand.

"Hello! Come on in, Melanie." Her black curls bounce as she turns and waves me into the room with the paintbrush.

How did she recognize who I was right away? Doesn't she have at least a hundred students in this dorm?

She grabs a paint palette from a small table. "Go ahead and find a place to sit. I'll be right with you." She disappears into a room which I assume is her bedroom.

The place resembles a mini apartment with its petite kitchenette. The stove and fridge hide in the corner with a dining table pushed against the wall. Two couches and a comfy-looking chair act as a living room. An easel sits in the corner with an unfinished landscape painted on the canvas. Every inch of wall space is crammed with art, specifically paintings, except for a charcoal drawing of three crucifixion crosses that's been framed. The paintings' subjects range from landscapes to Bible scripture painted in fancy yet readable script.

I close my eyes for a moment as I sit in the chair, the judgement seat, waiting for the reprimand and punishment. Kat and Harrison's warnings flit through my head. My eyes flutter open when Nikki comes back into the room with a pen and manilla folder.

"Okay. Let's get started. Most importantly, how are you feeling?"

I wipe my sweaty palms onto my leggings then rest my hands on my already bouncing knees. "I-uh. I'm starting to feel better."

"I'm glad to hear it. Also, for full disclosure, I have to report this incident to the housing department," Nikki comments as she sits cross-legged on the couch in front of me. She wears a gray T-shirt and black sweatpants cinched around the ankles instead of her apron. I notice her colorful fuzzy socks.

Her casual outfit contradicts the shame clasped deep in my chest.

Nikki appears thoughtful as she flips open her folder

and grabs out a piece of paper. "Well, I'll get right to it. No need to drag this out. You violated the school's alcohol policy."

I shake my head 'yes', wishing I was anywhere else. Time to face my decisions.

After a deep breath I ask, "Do you know who found me? I want to thank them."

Nikki clears her throat and reads through the report. "Your suitemate, Erin, said she heard a crash from your room and went to investigate with someone named Andre, another resident of this dorm. They found you unconscious on your bed, a bottle of vodka smashed on the ground, some vomit on the floor, and your window open with the screen missing. Other empty alcohol shots were around the room. She tried to wake you and when she couldn't, she called 911 while Andre contacted your RA Taylor and myself."

I rub my temple, feeling a headache starting and letting the information sink in. Erin and Andre, of course. The two people who are the nicest to me and never require anything in return are always with me at my worst.

I keep chasing after those who want Party Melanie. Drunk Melanie. "Sexy" Melanie. They don't want me as the true Melanie. When I fall, they are nowhere to be found. The people who care have been in front of my face this entire time, and I've brushed them off because of my desire for unconditional acceptance from anyone and everyone.

I really need to talk to Erin and Andre after this meeting.

Nikki interrupts my thoughts. "As far as punishment goes, our policies include a weekly room check until the end of the semester and your attendance of a sort of AA program for a few Saturdays. They have sessions on underage drinking, consequences of alcoholism, and give counseling." She pauses, making sure her last point is clear. "And if we find alcohol in your room again, you can be kicked out of the dorm or even the university."

I glance up at Nikki, her eyebrows furrowed. She sets the report and folder to the side. "My job is to make sure my residents are safe. But more than that, I care for you as a human." She uncrosses her legs and leans toward me. "So, I'm not saying this as some authority figure trying to tell you what to do. I say this as a peer who has been in your shoes."

She locks eyes with me. "It's supposed to be fun. The partying and all that. I did it too. But most people don't understand moderation. They take it as far as they can go because they're trying to fill a void, not enjoy themselves. They don't realize it either. In the end, it's poison."

I break eye contact, glancing above her and reading some of the words painted on a canvas: "The world and its desires pass away, but whoever does the will of God lives forever."

I study the words. *Wow, the irony. I bet she put it there on purpose to start conversations with visitors like me.*

Nikki follows my gaze to the canvas, her smile lighting up her whole face. "I know what some people say about me around here. They don't define me." She stands and walks over, extending her hand to me. I take it, and she helps me to my feet.

"But truly. If you need something, please talk to me. The point of my job is being here for you," Nikki insists as she places her hand on my shoulder.

I shift from foot to foot. "Thank you so much. I need to talk with Erin and Andre if you don't mind."

Nikki leads me out of her room, leaving me to ponder what happened to make her care that much for strangers.

Because that's what Jesus would do, of course.

Instead of running away from the problem, I reluctantly return to my room, back to where this mess started. The room is clear of the vomit and the bottle's glass shards, and the screen has been replaced in the window; no traces left of the night before. I wring my hands as I survey the scene of the crime. *I guess the missing screen was why I saw car headlights in my room last night. The window was open. Glad they fixed that. But who cleaned the mess?*

These observations lead me to the question I've been ignoring today: how did I get here? I know the answer already. It started the first day in this room. The spiral began from a mindset focused on myself and my loneliness, as if I am the only freshman struggling with this monumental life transition; when I isolated myself out of fear then ran after the first sight of something that looked like companionship; when I couldn't face life's stress and stuffed it so far down until it erupted. Last night was the pinnacle, the devastation left behind from my choices.

I sigh, setting my bag on the bed and grabbing my phone. I need to face Erin and Andre and apologize. Hopefully they won't be too mad at my dramatic antics yesterday. Hopefully they will forgive me.

I text Andre before knocking on Erin's bathroom door.

"Come in," she answers.

I tentatively enter her room even though I have permission. She has witnessed me at my lowest points this semester, but I know little about her personal life. A map of the world clings to her wall along with posters of various action/thriller movies. Medication bottles and dirty dishes line one desk while clothes promise an avalanche on her chair. DVD cases and books crowd a bookshelf. Erin is propped up in bed with her laptop. When she sees me, she crosses her arms over her stomach but keeps eye contact.

I stand in the doorway and wave. Where do I begin? She deserves this though. I have to be brave.

"How's it going?" I ask.

She pulls out her headphone's earbuds. "Oh, hey."

Of course, it's awkward. She found me unconscious. Gathering my courage, I take a step toward her. "Listen. I'll just say it. I've been a rotten person to you. I'm so sorry. Last night was serious and you handled it so well." I'm standing in the middle of the room, and her eyes are trained on me, unreadable. I don't look away from her even as she remains silent and watches me intently.

I smile. "Thanks for always being here for me. And if you don't mind, I would like to hang out with you and Andre more. Only if you want me to."

She exhales, and the tension in her posture slightly relaxes. "Apology accepted. It's hard for me to stay angry or hold grudges." She yawns and stretches. "Glad you're okay. That was some scary stuff."

"It was. Thanks for calling 911. Seriously."

"You're welcome. Don't do it again."

"You don't have to worry about that."

"Any kind of punishment?"

"Some kind of AA seminar for underage drinkers and room checks. I need it, apparently."

"We all have issues we're running from," she says with a shrug as she unwraps herself from her blankets and snatches car keys from the nightstand. "Well, wanna get dinner with me?"

I smile. "I'll pay tonight."

Turns out I can save a little bit of money when I'm not spending it all on alcohol.

Now I sit in Erin's car on the way to her favorite Asian restaurant according to her. The radio's music drowns out any chance of conversation, but this time it's not such a bad thing. I need this simplicity of two college girls eating dinner on a Saturday night, nothing less or more. I'll live right here in the present; allow the past and the future to remain hazy and unreachable in my mind.

This moment is enough for me.

Chapter 23

Sunday dawns bright, the last of the winter chill barely holding on. I sit in the second-floor lounge, sipping a cup of herbal tea and looking at the parking lot below. Andre responded to my text last night after Erin and I ate our ramen bowls and watched a movie. He's meeting with me after church today.

I haven't talked to him for months. He's not the only one I'm avoiding. Has he noticed? I'm polite at work, but any invitations to hang out with him and Erin are met with excuses. I won't be alone with Andre, but I say no anyway. Thankfully he is willing to meet me in the lounge, a public place.

I can't be alone in a room with any guy.

I hear Andre before I see him. He's humming as he walks up the stairs. Church must have been good today.

"Hey, you!" he says from behind my chair.

I jump, the tea sloshing but staying in the cup.

"Oh, shoot. Didn't mean to scare you," Andre apologizes as he sits in the chair across from me, placing a plastic bag on his lap. "Hope you don't mind me eating. Church went late as usual and I'm starving."

I shake my head. "I'm sorry. I heard you humming. I shouldn't have been so jumpy. And please eat. I shouldn't be too long."

"Apologizing for things that aren't your fault?" He teases as he pulls out a deli sandwich from the bag.

I take a deep breath and let it out slowly. "Well, this time it is my fault. I wanted to apologize to you in person. I've already talked to Erin, and she was so gracious." He sets his sandwich down in its paper wrapping, giving me his full attention. I continue, my voice shaky. "I'm so sorry. You've been a good friend for absolutely no reason since I've met you. And all I've done is abuse that kindness."

He leans forward, but I unconsciously shrink back into the chair. Andre notices my reaction. He sits back in his chair.

I look him in the eyes for the first time. "Can you forgive me for being a terrible person?"

He smiles but doesn't move closer to me. "I won't lie. It was stressful, but of course I forgive you. As random as it sounds, I do care about you." He shakes his head, amused. "It was your lame jokes at work probably. But really. I'm not mad. I wouldn't mind hanging out sometime too."

I stare into my tea, my stomach twisting into itself. I

want to be his friend and spend time with him. Dark memories play at the edges of my mind, and I try to shove them down. *Not now.*

"Melanie, are you okay? You're shaking a little."

I set my tea down and wrap my arms around myself, breathing in and out, trying to calm myself. *Don't dump your problems on him. You've done enough.*

Yet the words tumble out of my mouth, restrained for months but flowing freely. "I've been brushing you off lately. It's not you. Please, please understand that. You and Erin have been nothing but kind. But...I'm not ready to talk about what happened. Not yet." My breath is unsteady, tears blurring my vision despite the fact anyone could walk through the lounge.

"Thanks for explaining. And I should be the one apologizing about that. I noticed something wasn't right but didn't want to bug you. I should have at least asked. See something, say something you know?" He pauses, his forehead wrinkled in thought. "I want to be here for you, but if you need space, I respect that. These are real feelings. All I ask is that when you're ready, talk to someone. You deserve that."

I close my eyes, wishing the tears wouldn't fall. They do anyway.

Andre's voice breaks through my sudden turmoil. "Can I pray with you? Would that helpful?"

He's told me at work that he'll pray for me, when I've

briefly mentioned my stress, but this would be the first time he ever asked in person. I've been running for so long, and nothing is going right. Everything I've put my trust in has failed me. What could prayer hurt?

I open my eyes and sniffle, nodding at his offer. I glance at my hands, having seen people hold hands when they prayed at high school.

Andre smiles. "We don't have to hold hands. God hears us." He bows his head and closes his eyes. I mimic him, but my eyes remain open.

He begins. "Dear God, thank You for another day with You. We are grateful that You listen to us. You care about our hurt and our needs.

So, I pray for my friend Melanie. You know her and her pain. And You've been with her through everything. You promise that You're near to the broken-hearted and those crushed in spirit. Please be near Melanie and heal her heart. I pray she'd feel Your comfort and that You would strengthen her to be courageous, to do it afraid.

Calm her anxious heart with Your peace that's beyond our understanding. Thank You for Your faithful love for us. We humbly pray this in Your name, Amen."

It must be Andre's gentle tone or his intentional words, but my shaking stops during his prayer. He raises his head and makes eye contact with me, a grin on his face, as if he knew I would be calmer. He hands me a napkin from his food bag, and I blow my nose. It's quiet for a

259

moment; no one passed through the lounge, giving us the privacy I needed for this conversation.

I look him in the eyes. "Thank you."

"You're welcome. Do you want to be alone?"

I nod and he stands, grabbing his things. "I'm here when you're ready. And if I'm not the right person for you to talk to, that's okay too. I'll be praying for you regardless." He pauses in the doorway of the stairwell, turning his head. "If you ever want to hang out with Erin and me, the invitation is always there."

He disappears up the stairwell to his room. He's humming again. Always joyful, that one.

I turn back to the parking lot, my tea long cold. My thoughts never pick up and rage like they always do. That peaceful feeling Andre prayed for lingers. I can't deny it even if I don't believe in it.

What he prayed for is what I need. "Heal her heart," he had said. Yes, healing is next on my to-do list. I can't keep running because no matter what I do to avoid it, the memories will hunt me down. I'm not sure how healing will look. It will hurt, but I've been hurting myself all this time already.

Somewhere I'll find the courage to face everything I've been running from. It starts with one step at a time.

Chapter 24

First Weekend Meeting
April

"So, do you know why you're here, Melanie?" the middle-aged woman sitting across from me asks. The name tag pinned on her shirt tells me to call her Dr. Collins, a volunteer for this AA program designated for underage drinkers.

Well, for those who are caught.

I yawn, the coffee I chugged unsuccessful at waking up my brain for this 8 a.m. meeting on a Saturday. "I got caught drinking illegally and as punishment, I'm here," I reply as I adjust on the springy floral couch.

She gives a knowing smile, tapping her pen against her pad of paper. "Well, yes. But sometimes underage drinking is a sign of other kinds of distress that can be helped with therapy. That's where I come in."

My stomach twists. She'll pry into places I've blocked from everyone. I don't know what to say.

Dr. Collins continues despite my reluctance. "I'm a

volunteer for this program, and I'm here as a preliminary consultation to see if therapy would be beneficial for you."

I don't want to talk or think about any of it.

"Counseling is uncomfortable. So, I'll ask a question and let you talk. Say whatever you want. I might ask follow-up questions to guide our conversation."

I pick at my nails, trying to distract myself from the emotions rising to the surface. *I can do this. This is my first step toward healing. Acknowledgment and talking about my stress,* I remind myself hoping it will calm my frantic heartbeat.

It does not.

She proceeds. "So, tell me about your year. The first year of college is an adjustment for most students."

I swallow back the panic bubbling its way into my throat, but I manage to answer. "Yeah. I moved six hours away from home to a place full of strangers." I place my hands in my lap then continue. "It was nice to get away from my parents. Lots of drama recently. And my mom's marketing firm. She really wants me to take over the family business."

"Is this something that interests you?"

"Not at all."

"Is there something you want to do?"

I nod, not letting fear keep me from being honest. "Write. I enjoy writing. So, possibly journalism? News. I want to talk about the real stuff. Teachers and professors have told me I'm good at writing, and I'm observant."

Except when he led you into a bedroom alone.

My nails dig into my thighs. *Stop. Not now.*

Dr. Collin's pen stops. "You like writing, but you're a business major, correct?"

"Yeah. Having to tell my mom that and switching majors to something that might not pay the bills is terrifying." Letting my mom down and having enough money—these are only two of my worries.

I can stick with this path and be miserable or try to make something of my dreams. My doubts always get in the way. Shouldn't I buckle down like everyone else and get a business degree? Go home to a cat, have a warm meal, then do it the next day. And the next day. For the rest of my life until retirement.

I will waste away, unmotivated and numb.

Dr. Collins and I speak further about the family business and my relationship with my parents. I've had time to process and accept my parents' divorce, so it's easier to talk about with a stranger.

She clears her throat. "You put a lot of pressure on yourself to do what your mom expects. Make sure you find a way to let that pressure go in a healthy way."

"This is the part where you tell me not to drink anymore?"

She stands with an upturned lip. "Well, I won't say something you are already thinking."

We shake hands, and she explains that her assistant will email me about the next Saturday meeting. Dr. Collins is moving to the west coast to work at a nonprofit called the Recovery Center. She hands me a business card for counseling services in town without suggesting if I should go or not.

That choice is up to me.

The truth is that I'm not ready to talk about it. I'm not ready to let loose the pain I've shut away. I should go to therapy and talk about my problems, about my...experiences this year.

I need more time before that.

One would think after having a near-death experience, amongst other things, that therapy wouldn't sound so scary. Not living a life that suits my passions and not being myself frightens me the most. That's what I need to do: start living as me, myself, and I.

Whoever that is.

~ ~ ~

Another week comes and goes. I find myself alone in my bed on a Saturday night. My thumb hovers over my phone screen where social media will show people pregaming, posting their outfits before they go out for the night, and the madness of the bars. This is my bad habit when I'm bored and have nothing to keep my mind pre-occupied. I watch everyone living while I hide in the dorm.

Before I let any thoughts sabotage my night, I send a

group text message to Erin and Andre, asking if they want to hang out.

Wow. I'm getting brave. Well, brave-er.

Erin texts back: "Best timing ever. We are in the lobby about to leave for bowling."

Bowling? Is that considered athletic? I won't be any good at it. The last time I've bowled was at a middle school birthday party. But I can watch if I want to. Better than sitting in my room with an inevitable pity party on the horizon. Besides, the bowling alley isn't like the bars. It's safer, and I'm with people who care about me.

I change into athletic wear and sprint to the lobby before I can talk myself out of it. The sensation of running down the stairs is exhilarating.

No more heels for Melanie.

Erin, Andre, and a few faces I don't recognize crowd by the front desk. Erin's face lights up when she sees me.

"Yes! We can have a ladies vs guys game. Someone had cancelled last minute," she explains.

I cross my arms. "Oh, I'm not sure you want me on your team. I haven't played since—"

Andre holds up a hand. "I will not hear any negative talk about you tonight." He nudges my arm with his elbow. "Let's have some fun."

"Fine. I'll be kind to myself." I follow Erin and two other girls to her car while Andre takes the guys.

The bowling alley is down the main road, so we

arrive within minutes. Music and smoke greet us at the entrance, but the intensity doesn't compare to the bars and clubs. We put on our bowling shoes in the dim light while Andre orders pizza.

Erin waves me over to two open lanes next to each other. She explains, "Okay. Picking your ball is important. Gotta choose the right weight. If I were you, I would go with less weight since you're new. Start with a ten. Oh, and make sure your thumb is comfortable in it."

"Come here often?" I ask as I survey the bowling balls and choose a purple one.

Erin lifts a multicolored one for herself and sets it in the rack on the machine that returns the bowling balls; I follow her example.

"Yeah, my sister and I bowl for fun, so I'm here a few times a month to keep up my skills. Can't have her beating me when I go home," Erin explains as Andre returns with two large pizzas.

He sets them on the table. "Okay, people. We got 4 vs 4 tonight. The men folk vs ladies as requested by Erin. Winner gets epic bragging rights per usual," Andre says as he grabs a light blue ball and sets it in the machine along with the other guys' bowling balls.

"Do you want bumpers, Melanie?" He grins so big his eyes mischievously squint behind his glasses.

"Bumpers? No, I'll beat you without any handicaps," I say, my hands resting on my hips.

"Oh, you're competitive then?" he asks, a laugh following his question.

"I'm so competitive. I just suck at everything." That gets a chuckle from the group.

The game begins shortly after we have a slice of pizza. On my first turn, I walk up to the lane and lift the ball to my chest. My arms complain, sore from the arm workout I did yesterday, but I can't give Andre something to tease me about. Even mimicking Erin's swing fails; somehow, the ball falls into the guy's bowling lane next to ours and is immediately swallowed by the gutters.

I spin around, the lighting hiding my blush, to claps and laughter. I laugh along at my own mistake. Erin pats my shoulder as she grabs her ball from the ball return.

"You reconsidering those bumpers?" Andre taunts as I sit down.

"I'm getting warmed up," I say as I grab another slice of pizza.

Food after dinner and pizza of all things; making mistakes and laughing about it; hanging out with people that enjoy being with a sober me. I am safe. This could be how my life looks like from now on: eating whatever and whenever, having fun and remembering it, and no consequences like hangovers or hookup regrets.

Isn't this living—finding what you enjoy and clinging on to it; not just what you're trying to avoid or escape from; these little moments that make life worth living?

Chapter 25

On an unsuspecting Monday morning, a school-wide email is sent out before classes. I read the whole email, but the highlights stick out like a punch to the gut: *"Condolences to the family of lacrosse player, Isaac J. Williams...School memorial to be held on the lacrosse field this coming Friday. "*

What the email fails to mention finds me through the rumors spreading across campus during my morning and afternoon classes.

Found in his apartment room on Saturday morning.

A teammate discovered him.

The method.

On Friday morning, Isaac cracked jokes in our economics class like he always does. Isn't that what people always say? "He or she was the happiest person." My memories of him cascade through my mind. I helped Isaac with his Spanish homework before class last semester. We partied back in the day when I was in the team's good graces and occasionally ate meals with him and the team. He played lacrosse so well.

We are acquaintances, but we share space and experiences; I learn of his passing through an email, such an impersonal way. *I'm not close to them anymore. Why would anyone text me about it? But speaking of team…*

I don't think twice as I send Dylan a text message asking him if he's okay. Of course, he's not. But I say I tried. His number remains in my phone, but he doesn't respond. Not sure why I felt it appropriate to text him after all these months.

Maybe because he wasn't doing well the last time I saw him.

I return to the dorm room after lunch and a morning of unfazed classes. It's cruel. Life goes on, but that doesn't make it right or easy. Erin watches me from the open bathroom door as I fall into my unmade bed.

Standing in the bathroom doorway, she sighs. "I'm guessing you saw the email. So sad. Did you know him? You were close to the lacrosse team for a while," she says.

"Yeah," are the only words I can get out without crying.

She remains by the door, giving me the space I need. "I'll go with you to the school memorial on Friday if you want. Might be good to have a buddy, and I wanna pay my respects too," she says.

I turn my head towards her. "I appreciate you. We can meet here and walk together."

She somehow understands my dismissive tone. Erin

waves, and leaves me to ruminate like I do best.

Do I deserve to be sad? Isaac and I are practically strangers. I don't know what makes him happy, his secrets, his story, and the darkness that led him away.

So, I'm stuck doing seemingly pointless actions: pacing, reading the messages of condolences and encouragement on his social media and writing one of my own, and wishing I had done more. Anything.

How human of me.

Despite my history with the team, I shove my pride aside and go with Erin to the field late Friday afternoon. Chairs and flowers surround a stand with a framed picture of Isaac playing lacrosse, of course. An older woman and man sit to the left—bent, curled into themselves. The team and close friends stand by their chairs at the front, facing his picture. Dylan's curly hair isn't hard to miss; there's no team hats or jerseys in sight. I sink into a chair in the back with Erin at my side.

I glance to my right and notice someone in the same row as us, in the corner furthest away from everyone. It's Lauren. She wears a modest black outfit, her signature ponytail combed out into natural waves. There are no traces of her flawless makeup; only tears streaming down her puffy face.

I was always jealous of her body, confidence, and popularity. But here she is, alone, crumbling in grief with no one to comfort her. Harrison, others, and I placed her on a pedestal like a trophy as the shiny model college student. Yet, she's only human like the rest of us. Grieving and in need of support through this sorrow.

I hope she finds peace.

The mournful silence soaks into my bones. Everyone sits then the coach and some teammates say a few words through their tears and sobs. Isaac's father thanks us for honoring Isaac's memory. His mother can't speak. Students come in waves to the front after the service and disappear gradually like a creeping tide; many will set down their grief on this field. My attention fixes on his family, his teammates, and close friends. Even Lauren. They don't get to leave these feelings behind.

I'm frozen in my chair. I have no obligation to this team, surely. But there's the right thing and the easy thing. I know what I should do—focus on someone else for once, for those who can't forget this tragedy. I would want someone to do the same if it were me.

Erin is the brave one. She stands, and we walk to the front row, speaking briefly and politely with his parents. We remain next to the team and Isaac's friends; the team's usual rambunctious laughter and carefree demeanor contrasting their present black attire and unabashed tears.

Dylan sits close by hands clutching his face. Ben stands next to him with a hand on Dylan's shoulder.

I hear Dylan whimper into his hands as he speaks to Ben. "Why did I have to find him?"

The words are another punch to the gut.

Dylan found Isaac.

Ben leans down and says something to him that I can't hear. Dylan responds with, "I should have known. Anything I do, it's never enough, man…"

Is this how Isaac felt? Never feeling enough, even though he was surrounded by people who loved him? If that's the case, who have I been ignoring, so wrapped up in my own problems to notice their suffering?

I'm brought out of my reverie by Dylan coughing. Ben offers him a tissue that Dylan ignores. Guilt and regret are ruthless beasts. Dylan will always remember this. I can't find the right words, my mind swirling with possibilities; none of my ideas feel enough or sincere. A dull ache settles in my head.

When Dylan finally drops his hands, he grabs a tissue from the box beside him and blows his nose. He doesn't notice me but stares somewhere across the field. His gaze is empty and unintentional. Most of the team mirrors his posture. I want to help them, so I don't feel utterly powerless. What could I possibly do for them? Nothing I say or do will bring him back.

I'm not God.

They will find ways to cope; some of those choices are positive, others destructive. It will need to heal on its own—this open wound that seals through time and processing but will linger; grief always leaves a scar. They will have to face their regret and sorrow if they want to heal. They'll have to face their pain, unlike what I'm doing.

The teammates are asked to remove the chairs, and his parents rapture Isaac's picture and the flowers. Erin quietly chats with another student while I help fold and stack the chairs. Dylan stops next to me.

He clears his throat. "Thanks for being here. You didn't have to."

I nod, not trusting my mouth. If I'm not careful, I'll end up apologizing for something or say something sarcastic. We stand in silence for a long moment.

"Were you the freshman found unconscious in their dorm?" he asks.

His question catches me off guard. I press my lips together then somehow manage a deflated, "Yeah."

He grimaces. "I heard rumors. You know how everyone is here. They talk. Then…this happens."

"I'll be okay, Dylan. I promise. Don't worry about me."

He shakes his head. "I'll probably worry about everyone I know for the rest of my life."

"Talk with someone. You don't have to carry this alone. You have people that care about you."

He shrugs. "I know. This isn't the first time."

I'm not angry at his dismissal of the only kind words I've said to him in months. I get it. Grief is a long, winding road. We have things to work through, but that journey will not be taken with each other.

Perhaps someday Dylan and I can do what I wanted from the start: go on dates and tell each other our pasts, our secrets without fear; talk about the hard stuff. That's the naive optimist in me who wishes life didn't have to be complicated; a life where Dylan can be a committed boyfriend, and I have the love I long for but haven't found yet.

Instead of replying, I watch as Dylan walks into the field with his teammates, the sun sluggishly dipping into the horizon and casting long shadows against the withered grass.

~ ~ ~

The day after the ceremony, my melancholy hasn't abated. Not wanting to be alone, I knock on Erin's door. A noise sounds from the room, which I interpret as permission to enter. What I see shocks me. A single bulb in the lamp illuminates the room, dishes cover the desk while a mountain of trash and crumpled papers circle their attempted target. In the corner, laundry seeps out of the hamper.

A bundle of blankets on the bed moves; Erin has cocooned herself within them. I've been hanging out with Erin and Andre recently, but I can't recall the last time I've been in her room. I don't remember it being this messy.

"Erin?" I ask, still taking everything in.

"Huh?"

"Are you sick?"

"Not exactly."

I push past the awkwardness. "Can I help you clean up?"

She sighs. "You don't have to. I'll get to it."

"You're okay. I want to help. Please tell me what to do."

I ask Erin if I can text Andre about the situation, and she mumbles in agreement. He responds immediately and knocks on Erin's door soon after his reply. *Always ready to help someone*, I think as I let him in the room. For the next thirty minutes or so, Erin gives us minimum instructions; we tidy the room until it is almost spotless.

Erin creeps out of the covers when we finish cleaning, and I notice the dark circles under her eyes. She must have covered them with makeup at the funeral yesterday. She avoids eye contact as she escapes into the bathroom and shuts the door.

"Should I be concerned?" I ask Andre.

He motions for me to follow her, so I sit outside the door. She's sniffling and breathing deeply.

"Erin. You probably want us to leave you alone but I'm here to listen. If you need that," I tell her.

"It's been a rough few weeks. Well, months really." she admits.

"Any reason why?"

There's a long pause before she confesses, "Been struggling with classes. I stopped attending my morning statistics class because I couldn't get out of bed and the class was so hard for me. Guess the depression is kicking my butt."

I take a breath and quietly exhale, choosing my next words carefully. "You're brave to talk about that. I mean it. Not many people do." Andre is listening but is keeping a polite distance.

Erin blows her nose before saying, "I didn't want you seeing me differently. I don't want this to define me."

"Then don't let it. This is nothing to be ashamed about."

She opens the door. Erin opens her arms, and I give her the most present hug I can give.

"Thanks. It's been a heck of a time," Erin says as we separate.

"Anything we can do for you?" I ask as we return to her room.

She sniffles. "I'll have to repeat the class since it's required for my psychology major. Attendance counts for the grade, so I'll take it later in the day next semester. No more early morning classes for me."

She gives a half-hearted laugh. Andre places his hand on Erin's shoulder and gives it a squeeze. It's clear he's been walking through this with her.

Erin explains as if reading my thoughts, "Andre and

I have been talking and I'm gonna go to the doctor about it. See if it's something that needs counseling or some other form of long-term help." She gestures toward the medication bottles on her dresser. "Clearly, whatever I'm taking isn't helping me."

I wrap my arms around myself. "I'm proud of you. Not everyone gets the help they deserve."

She's doing what I'm too scared to do: getting help.

Andre's stomach grumbles, and the three of us laugh, the seriousness of the moment lost.

"Not to brush this under the rug but pizza? Tacos? Hamburgers? It is Saturday night, and the night is still young," Andre says.

"You can never go wrong with tacos." Erin's grin finally reaches her eyes.

Andre smiles. "Tacos it is. I'll drive."

After Erin changes her clothes, we pile into his truck for the local taco joint down the street. The country music from the truck's speakers swaddles us in acoustic guitars and banjos. I watch Erin as she leans her head against the window. All this time struggling alongside me, and I didn't realize because I was too busy being concerned about myself only.

How strong someone must be to keep moving forward even when their own feet are dragging, and no one notices.

Just like Dylan…and even Kat.

Just like Isaac had for a time.

Just like me.

Everyone is fighting internal battles, hoping someone else notices the smoke.

So in that car sitting with two people who are slowly but surely becoming my best friends, I decide something. I will start noticing. I will look for the signals. I can't help everyone, but I can try my best. That's something worth doing. That's something worth living for.

Chapter 26

Beginning of May

"Alright, Melanie. We are staging an intervention. Right here. Right now," Erin declares as she bursts through the door of the first-floor lounge. Andre joins her, mimicking her crossed arms and wide-legged stance like they are some security team duo.

I look up from my laptop and pull out my earbuds. "Shoot. What did I do?"

Andre wags his finger. "We're serious. You are too smart and awesome to be sitting around and hating life."

I shut the algebra textbook, realizing this is not a complete joke. They move closer to me but give me some space.

"You're clearly unhappy and it's something you can change," Andre explains.

"You hate your major, you're overworked, and you don't wanna own the family business. What are we doing about this?" Erin asks.

The "we" statement makes me smile. I have people

watching out for me now.

I shrug. "Well, I'm glad you pay attention. I guess…I want the change, but I'm afraid."

Andre sits next to me. "What do you fear, Mel?" He stopped calling me CEO once we discussed I, in fact, didn't want to be a CEO.

I cringe at the nickname but answer, "I've made so many mistakes lately. What if I fail?"

"Well. I suppose you make the changes and if it sucks, you keep trying until it doesn't." Erin sits as well. "But you'll never know if you don't try. You're already miserable. It can only go up from here, right?" She smiles with all her teeth, and I laugh.

"Do it afraid," Andre comments with one of his many catchphrases.

I hold up my hands in defeat. "Okay, fine. Give me some time to think about it, and I'll get back to you with some ideas."

Andre pumps his fist. "Misson accomplished. Time for food."

"Wait a minute. This can't be all about me. What about you two?" I try to stare menacingly at them but end up grinning. "Good changes for the three of us. How about that?"

"Oh, fine. But first, let's go get some food," says Erin as she bounds out the door.

Andre stands. "No rush. She's excited as usual. We'll

wait for you in the lobby."

I collect my things, letting my mind drift to our conversation. What will my life look like if I decide to do what I want? Not what Mom expects nor what my peers or society think is proper.

What am I made for?

I'll find out by thinking–no, enough of that–by daydreaming without the doubt that inevitably creeps in. Erin and Andre are here to help me wade through that insecurity until I learn to stand on my own two feet.

And I hope to do the same for them.

As Andre keeps saying to me, "Do it afraid." So that's exactly what I'll do. I'll do it afraid.

~ ~ ~

I sit cross-legged on the couch across from Erin at the welcome desk. I'm hunched over my laptop, fingers hovering. Frozen. Afraid.

"This is one of the last steps you gotta take to get your life back on track. You can't quit on me now," Erin insists between bites of her microwave mac and cheese. "Besides, I already applied to be a Resident Advisor, and we shook on it. You can't bail."

The conversation–more like subtle intervention–earlier in the week initiated the major life decision avalanche I'm running with now because they're right. I am miserable but have some agency. After giving each other time to think, we talked through a plan to make positive changes in our lives; we can only control so much but being proactive and accountable to each other can only help our chances of changing our lives for the better, even in small ways.

And everyone knows I like to be in control with a clear, concise plan.

Erin mentions counseling and talking with a psychiatrist about the depression episodes she finds herself in often. Andre ditches wearing the formal clothing all the time because "he was trying too hard to impress people who don't care." He also wants to go to the gym regularly for health reasons, leading the three of us to become gym buddies. It's nice to have people in the gym with me, so I don't obsess over cardio and trying to "earn" the calories I eat.

Finally. I admit what I was doing to myself.

I quit admissions along with Andre. I need another job that pays more than the minimum wage that admissions gave us, which leads me to the next step: applying for a Resident Advisor job with Erin. When I'm not doing something for the dorm like planning events and room checks, I can do homework during the "office hours" where I must be in my room anyway for the residents to stop by if they need something; it seems like the perfect way to balance my time between work, school, and relaxation.

Leaning over my laptop, my fingers remember their

function, and I thoughtfully fill out the job application until it's complete. I hit submit before I can talk myself out of it. Erin cheers then covers her mouth since it's eleven o'clock at night.

Next is addressing my major and telling Mom about the new plans for my future education and career, the most frightening task. At least I have supportive friends helping me through and keeping me accountable. If it wasn't for them, I'd overthink myself from doing any of this.

~ ~ ~

I sit in my academic advisor's office and observe the intimidating wall of business books behind his wrinkled face. He glances from the paper in front of him to me, and I muster the most confident expression I can. I'm sure he sees right through my façade.

He clears his throat. "You're switching majors?" he asks.

I nod, searching for words. What explanation do I owe this guy? I sit taller. "Yes. This is a better career path for me."

"Communications major with journalism and creative writing minors? That's a harder field to get into, and the pay is less. You haven't thought this through. You are only a freshman."

I've heard it before. I mentioned being interested in writing to my high school counselor. Her response matched his. In the end, everything revolves around that number in my bank account and the lake house that sits empty because I'm too busy working to enjoy it. I shouldn't pursue my passions because it's childish. Naive. I need to grow up.

I'll have to prove them wrong. Including myself since doubt is creeping into my stomach, making me want to throw up. That will make quite a statement, but also be an embarrassing story that will find its way around campus. I better be careful.

"I've considered all of this. Business is for some people, but not for me. Money will come somehow." I say without hesitation.

He shakes his head, focusing somewhere above my head. "Good luck with your endeavors, I suppose."

This is how I expected the conversation to go.

Now to tell Mom. From one giant to the next. If I stop then fear and doubt will drag me back down. Telling my mom is terrifying enough. Her opinion of me matters more than it should.

Back at my dorm, I wait to video call her until 5:30 p.m., her minuscule pause after dinner and before planning the schedule for tomorrow's workday.

Two heads appear through the open bathroom door.

"Tell her who's boss. You're the CEO of your life!" Erin cheers.

"And that you still love her even though she might not respect your decisions," Andre concludes as they disappear back into her room, waiting for the results of my conversation.

I laugh and press the button to video chat. My breath almost forgets to leave my nostrils when her face appears on my phone screen.

"Good evening. You've caught me at a good time. I finished dinner, and I was about to prepare my schedule for tomorrow," Mom says.

She's predictable at least.

"How's it going?" I ask, my mind ciphering through hundreds of ways to begin this conversation and its possible conclusions.

"Well, we landed a new client that I've been going in circles with for months, but we secured a deal and—"

"I dropped my business major," I blurt out as all the trains of logical ideas in my mind derail.

That's one way to do it.

"Excuse me?" she asks.

I start over. "I dropped my major to study—"

"Melanie, you need a business major. Your degree will ensure people will take you seriously as a business professional."

"I'm majoring in communications with journalism and creative writing minors now."

"Journalism?"

"Yes, I want to be a writer. A reporter. Whatever that is like years from now."

Her face magnifies on the screen as she leans in. "You're giving up the family business? You're throwing that away?"

I brace myself, raising my shoulders and leveling my chin. "Your business, Mom. You've built a great company, but I won't be the one taking it over. Did you ever ask what I wanted?"

She looks away from her phone. "Well, no. But it's a great opportunity that most people your age won't get until they are my age."

"Well, I'm making my own decisions. It's just not what you want from me."

She throws her hands up. "After all I've done for you."

"I'm learning what it means to make my own choices. This is my decision. Not yours. Not Dad's. Mine."

"Did this mean nothing to you?"

I exhale probably too loudly. "It means a lot that you would build this so I could take it over. But you didn't consider if I was the right person."

She finally looks at me.

"I'm not the right person, business major or not. I'll see you in a few weeks for the summer, okay? We can talk more about it then."

"Fine. Bye, Melanie."

The screen goes blank, and I jump on my bed like I'm

five years old again. I did it. I made these decisions on my own. I did it afraid. Andre and Erin run into the room to join my celebration with cheers and laughter, a feeling I never want to forget.

Freedom.

~ ~ ~

"I knew you would come around, Melanie," Dr. Slate sheepishly grins from behind his desk. Pieces of art crowd every inch of his office walls and the bookshelves buckle with every classic literature piece I can name and more.

I shrug. "Business isn't for me."

"Better now than later. I wasted many years pursuing corporate work, and I've nothing to show for it."

I slide the paperwork for my official major change and minor additions, and Dr. Slate signs it. The lack of hesitation on my behalf shocks me, but it only proves further how I craved a change even if I could not fully admit it to myself or do anything about it.

"I'm assuming your previous advisor gave you some talk about how you won't make money, correct?" He looks down his glasses at me, but that knowing grin remains.

"Mom hinted at the same thing," I answer without pausing. Speaking what I think—what a revolutionary concept.

He clasps his hands together. "Maybe they are right. It's not always a simple path for us writers and some don't make it. But that's the thrill. Trying, failing, trying again, and succeeding. Quite the adrenaline cycle."

"I'm guessing rejection is a big part of this whole thing?"

His gaze is fixed on me, but he is not present for a moment as if he's recalling those moments of letdown. He nods, and his gaze returns to the present.

"Countless no's will find you in any field you go into. Some will hurt worse than others. Just–metaphorically, of course–burn the rejection slip and use that as motivation to keep trying."

"What if rejection and I don't get along?"

"You'll learn. Go for it, and you'll surprise yourself with how much easier it gets."

"You're right. I appreciate the advice."

He hands me the signed form then holds his hand out. "Welcome to the program. I'll see you in the Intro to Writing Creative Fiction class in August."

I grasp his hand harder than I should shake a professor's hand, but without another thought, I float out of his office, feeling more free than I have since I moved here.

Chapter 27

The Week Before Finals

I stand at Nikki's door, my hands sweating and my heart racing. The last time I was here had worse implications but that doesn't stop my nerves; nothing does. Nikki emailed Erin and I about interviews for the RA position. Erin had hers yesterday and said it went fine. "Don't sweat it" she said trying to comfort me. *Well, too late Erin. Interviews aren't simple matters for overthinkers.* But she's right.

I knock and Nikki opens the door. She's already holding a clipboard with what I assume are interview questions.

"I'm prepared for you this time." She laughs. "Come on in! Make yourself comfortable."

She waves me into her room where I'm welcomed by instrumental music and the smell of lavender and something like a hint of orange. She taps her phone, and the music stops. I settle into the cushioned chair like last time, and one of my knees bounces up and down. Nikki sits on the couch across from me.

"I'm diffusing oils for a calming effect. Interviews are scary for most people. Let me know if the smell ever gets too much," she explains, pointing to the little machine in the corner puffing scented mist into the air.

She's very aware of others. She would be a good boss.

I shake my head and try to smile, not wanting to say more than I need to. I don't ruin this from the start.

She crisscrosses her leg. "Perfect! Okay, let's get started. So, I received your application for the Resident Advisor job. We have a few job openings. But I wanted to tell you right away that the university does take this opportunity seriously."

Darn. I'm already thinking about my alcohol violation, my one big mistake. *Is she doing this interview out of obligation or am I'm truly a contender?*

She continues. "Especially since you marked you wanted to be in a freshman dorm where many of the students are more nervous, vulnerable, and might want someone as a friend or at least a peer that can answer their questions."

I blurt out, "That's exactly why I applied." I put my hand over my mouth.

Nikki laughs as she sets her pen down and leans closer. "That's awesome. Not a lot of people purposely seek out being an RA of a freshman dorm. They usually want a more 'chill' placement among peers the same age or slightly older. Tell me more about that, please."

I sit up straighter and begin my rehearsed speech.

"Well, I know exactly how the freshmen feel. I came here and was lonely and had questions, but I was too prideful or scared to ask." Nikki writes on her sheet as I continue. "So, I want to be that person they are comfortable talking to. Because I've been in their shoes before, and I know what it's like. I want to help them however I can. Because I needed that."

"And you feel you are up to the challenge?"

I set my hands on my knees, willing them not to bounce. "Yes. I am working on my people-pleasing tendencies, but this is the perfect opportunity to learn how to do that. And I'm friendly, I think."

"You're a recovering people-pleaser too? Welcome to the club. I've been in the exact same place before. Good job for recognizing that." Nikki marks up the page. "So, basically empathy is your main motivation for this role?"

"Yeah, I believe so. I don't really care to boss anyone around because I'm older than them."

"Well, it sounds like you've put a lot of thought into this. The role can be something to put on your resume. But if you want, you can use it to make a positive difference in someone's life."

I answer without hesitation, "That's the goal."

Nikki uncrosses her legs, placing her feet on the ground and the clipboard in her lap. "Well, do you have any questions about—"

"Am I disqualified because of my alcohol violation?"

Nikki shakes her head, which takes the edge off my nerves. "I wouldn't have set up an interview if it did. I know the housing office frowns upon those, but I can't be too harsh about one violation," she clarifies.

"Because that was you, right?" That question is probably too casual for an interview, so I quickly add, "If that's too personal you don't have to…"

"I'm open about that part of my life. I was partying and drinking and getting in trouble. Then I found a different path that addressed all the reasons I was over-indulging. Found freedom, joy, and hope. The things I was searching for in all the wrong places."

"Honestly, I heard about you briefly from a few other students. Some of the older ones," I admit.

Nikki's smile falters. "I see. Did Kat find you too?"

I wonder about Nikki's word choice.

Nikki crosses her arms. "As long as I've known Kat, she was always finding the lonely people and making them…feel less alone. At least for a time, that is." She breaks eye contact with me.

Why is Nikki saying something nice about Kat when Nikki clearly understands Kat is selfish? No one can be Kat's "friend" long before realizing the truth. She uses people.

Wow, I sound bitter.

Nikki interrupts my thoughts. "Well, I won't go into

that. It's in the past. What I'm trying to say is, I can't be judgmental about you breaking the rules when I did the exact same thing. I ask that you're honest with me and don't break them again if I decide to hire you. I like a staff that lives with integrity. But I hold myself to the same standard as well."

"Haven't had a drop of liquor since then." My confession feels more private than professional. When did this interview become so personal? Not that I mind. She's being vulnerable as well.

"Of course, you're nineteen. And when you're old enough, moderation can be just as fun."

I sigh once more with relief. "That was my only pressing concern about the job. I can handle the job duties and come back early in the fall to help with dorm set up and the trainings too."

Nikki's demeanor returns to her usual self: calm and causal. Any tension from our short conversation about Kat and Nikki's past is long gone. She makes a few more notes on the paper.

"Well, if you don't have any further questions, I'll go ahead and let you go. I'll get back to you either way by the beginning of next week." She stands, extends her hand, and I shake it.

"Thanks for your honesty, Melanie. It was a nice getting to know you more." She walks me to the door. "Oh, and I'll be praying for you and your finals next week.

You got this," she adds.

"Thanks for interviewing me and…for the prayers. I'm going to study now."

When the door shuts, I pump my fist into the air, not caring who is in the room. *That went well. Better than any interview I've had.* I'll study for finals and wait for her decision. Whatever she decides, what's important to me is that for the first time in forever, I'm proud of myself.

Chapter 28

Last Week Of School

Erin barges into my room, holding her laptop triumphantly over her head. I'm sitting on my bed, studying the notecards sprawled across the comforter. I jump at her sudden entrance, and a small pile falls to the floor.

She yells, "I got the email! I got the RA job!" I give her a purposeful blank stare, and her face becomes pink. She stammers, "Oh. Did you not get the same acceptance email? I mean, you're a perfect fit for the role and I can't believe they—"

I burst into laughter. "Erin. Heck yes, I got it! We're co-workers and roommates. Fourth floor of Montgomery Hall this fall."

Erin sets her laptop on the only empty spot on my desk since it's cluttered with other studying materials for final's week. She sits down and puts her feet up on the desk. "Gonna be funny. Us sophomores bossing freshmen around like we are so much older than them."

I grab the notecards from the floor then shuffle them to quiz myself for the hundredth time. "Well, working in this dorm is what we wanted, right? To be able to help them through their first year."

"You right. Look at us being model citizens."

"Speaking of model citizens, where's Andre?"

Erin shrugs. "I think he's been studying, too. Haven't seen too much of him this last week. Shall we go bug him?"

"We shall."

We jog up the stairs and to his door, playfully knocking a few times each. *Hopefully he's not taking a nap.* The door flings open as I'm going in for one more knock. Andre is wearing sweats, and I do a double take. He took his promise seriously and isn't wearing business casual on a random Monday in the dorm like he used to.

He motions for us to enter his room. I hesitate for a second. I take a deep, shaky breath and follow them in anyway. They either don't notice or don't mention it.

I'm safe here.

"I question your friendship sometimes. You bring out the annoying in each other," he mumbles as he turns on more lights to reveal a messy room, which seems unlike him. "Roommate moved out to live with his girlfriend awhile back. Had the place to myself ever since. Been too busy to clean recently."

Either he's a mind-reader or my face truly tells all.

"Dude. Melanie and I got the RA job! Let's go celebrate tonight. Tacos are the best option, but we could see a movie or drive around. Anything really," Erin gushes in excitement.

Andre shakes his head. "I have to get good grades this semester, and I have a few classes that were hard and—"

I put a hand on my hip. "Okay, what's really going on here?"

He sighs. "I mean it's true. I've been thinking about my purpose in life too. We have these big decisions about our futures hanging over our heads."

Erin sinks into his comfortable gaming chair. "Yeah. No big deal, right? Wrong. You're always helping others. It's our turn. What's up?"

He leans against the wall with his arms crossed. "I wanted to be a lawyer for as long as I can remember. I vowed 'no ministry for me'. Did I want to be different than my father and grandfather? Or show people I could earn something, so it wouldn't seem like things were handed down to me?"

Erin's mouth gapes open. "Wait. You're not going to be a lawyer?"

"That's the issue. For so long I've dismissed ministry. I wanted to do something important 'in the real world'. My own pride keeping me blind to things."

"What made you start thinking about this?" I ask.

"Honestly, after being here and seeing all trauma and

pain everyone endures, I want to help people through that. But I want it to be deeper than emotional help. What about the spiritual side of things?"

"Come on. Tell us. The anticipation is killing me," Erin pleads, her knees bouncing.

Andre gives us a half smile. "I'm figuring it out. But I might get degrees in ministry and counseling. So, I have the best of both worlds."

Erin's eyes light up. "A counselor? I would pay you to tell me how to feel better."

I've seen the way he has counseled Erin during the school year; the times he spent sitting at the front desk with her, talking her through the overwhelm and stress of college. She isn't the only one. I've seen him deep in conversation with several students around campus.

"You'll make a great counselor. Or pastor. Whatever you choose, you'll do it well," I encourage.

His half grin turns into a full smile. "Okay, okay. I take back what I said. You two, as friends, are a nice thing. I appreciate you both." His stomach growls, interrupting the sentimental moment. Andre laughs. "Well, why don't I call up some of my buddies, and we can get food? An arcade bar just opened that has food and mocktails."

Erin cheers, launching herself from the chair and out the door, leaving Andre and I alone.

"Hey, thanks for listening," Andre says.

I smile despite the nerves erupting in my stomach.

"Well, you and Erin have made being on campus a lot less horrible. It's the least I can do."

"You're right. Everyone needs support, even me. But we're doing hard things to make our lives better. I'm proud of us."

Which reminds me of something.

"Hey. You've really encouraged me to start caring for myself." I step closer until I'm standing right in front of him. "And I wanted you to know that I'm seeing a counselor this summer. To talk about things."

Maybe I imagine it, but I think I see a few tears brimming in his eyes.

"You're braver than you think, Melanie. You'll get through this and be a role model for your residents next year. Better yet, a good friend."

I open my arms for a hug, my heart pounding.

He takes a step toward me. "You okay with it?"

"Yeah."

He wraps his arms around me, keeping enough distance so I don't feel more uncomfortable than I already am. But this moment is important.

I whisper, "Thanks for being faithful to your God and acting like Jesus did in all those stories I read in school. It's changed my life for the better."

Andre gives me a quick squeeze, and we separate. "He's changed my life too. I would love to tell you about it when...if you ever want to talk about it." He sniffles and pushes his glasses back onto his nose. "Alright, I better get ready. I'll see you at dinner."

I don't wonder about his quick dismissal; it is probably from the suddenness of that emotional moment. It is important to me though. I wanted to tell him how I feel and not be afraid to hug a guy or be alone with him. It doesn't solve everything I've been through. It's more complicated than that.

I did it afraid. And that's a step in the right direction—forward.

I return to my room and as I brush my hair, a smile rises to my lips and melts my nerves until I'm relaxed. The last month has been a whirlwind of change. It's positive changes this time though; an impending new job and major and real friends like my own found family. None of which was by accident. I made major life decisions with the encouragement of two awesome people by my side.

I make other changes that I don't explain to Andre and Erin.

I unfollow Kat, Dylan, Dani, and the rest of my so-called friends on social media and delete their numbers. I keep Hayley and Alex's contacts. I don't blame them for the way we drifted apart this year. Our friendship might come back around, but I'll be okay if it doesn't.

I cut up my fake ID.

I donate the clothes that I wore to feel better about myself, even though I never felt better in them. Goodbye high heels.

I throw away my scale. I could have donated it, but the trash can feels more cathartic.

I schedule an appointment with a counselor in my hometown for this summer.

I've made tough choices lately, and I'm proud of that. I need to face some experiences that I haven't been able to talk about yet. I'll have to confess what I've buried during the school year. Right now, the thought of saying those things aloud makes my gut twist in knots.

But I'll do it anyway.

After what I've been through, I'm done running and burying my reality and experiences. I'm ready to try—to stop putting on a perfect mask for the world and pretend I have it all together; I'm ready to bear my trauma and imperfections–to the right people–and for that to be okay and enough.

I'm ready to be myself no matter who loves me or who loves me not.

Epilogue

May 15th, 2015

Our empty dorm room reminds me of a jail cell: neutral colors and echoes. About a week ago, Sophia collected her fluffy decor and disappeared with nothing more than a goodbye. I have finals until Friday, and my last day of freshman year finds me with As, Bs, and Cs in my classes. Those grades will have to be enough for me even if they weren't for Mom.

The last of my bags crowd the doorway, ready to be snatched up as I put this place behind me. I'll be back this fall to start my sophomore year of college and new job while promising to see that new action movie with Erin. We also assured Andre that we will join him a few cities over for their "actual college football game".

And both are willing to accompany me to the local renaissance faire.

I pause before I leave, letting that déjà vu feeling wash over me, and I welcome a flashback to my first day here. I walked through the doors of Montgomery Hall Room 219 naive to what the year would bring. It's cliché to say I learned a lot, but I cannot deny the truth behind it.

I'm learning to say no. To not be a "yes girl", everyone's shadow or doormat, ready to give whatever they need or want at the continual expense of myself. That's not how anyone makes or keeps true friends and healthy relationships. I'm learning to speak for myself and to be honest about what I've seen and experienced; to face uncertainty with confidence and accept that I don't have control of everything or know what the future holds.

That's the beauty of it, this mystery of the future. I don't know what will happen. I haven't figured it out yet. It's terrifying and dreadful but wonderful.

What do I know?

I'll live in the present, one foot in front of the other. As me. That's my next step: finding myself. Not whoever anyone decides I am; not the character I play to get people to like me. I'll be Melanie as I figure out who she is. I will honor the specific way I am made.

To thine own self, I will be true.

Here's to the other side of university with my grad cap, diploma, and the stories from the years I spent studying and living life to the fullest. I'll be standing on that stage, ready to face whatever life brings me after graduation.

I'll see you when I get there.

Acknowledgments

This book almost never came to be. But where a dream is, there's a dreamer fighting against the odds to do what they love to do.

First, I'd like to thank my husband. You'll probably never read this (and I don't blame you), but your loyalty and love are a blessing. You'll be my anchor, and I'll be your (chicken) wings forever. I love you.

Thank you to my dear friend and first writer/author companion, Rachel, for her encouragement and friendship. You are an answer to prayer.

To my family and friends for their support of this childhood dream and putting up with book marketing and my scheming and shenanigans. Sorry not sorry.

To Amanda, Anna, Claire, and Ashley for being my "found family" in college. I miss you and wish you the best in life.

Thank you to the classmates and professor who were in my Young Adult literature class in 2017. You had to listen to a short and nervous junior give a book proposal about a freshman named Melanie. She's finally made it off my computer screen and on to literal pages!

To God who has sustained, loved, and blessed me more than I deserve or can imagine. All glory forever.

And finally to Melanie, the woman that I was. We made it. We made it to that graduation stage and beyond. It wasn't easy, but we did it. I'm so proud of us.

Also By M.M. Bylo

<u>Poetry</u>

The Silent Advocate

Surviving The In-Between

Through The Long, Dark Night

Not Of This

M.M. Bylo resides in the Midwest with her husband and their rescue cat, Luna. Professionally speaking, she has written poetry, short stories, and novellas since the age of ten and minored in Creative Writing in college. In reality, all she dreams about is using her love of storytelling and her own experiences to share the love of Christ and encourage others. You can find her snuggled in blankets and fuzzy socks with a book or video game, wandering the outdoors, or trying to convince her perfectionist brain that rest is productive. University is her first novel.

www.ingramcontent.com/pod-product-compliance
Lightning Source LLC
Chambersburg PA
CBHW020408260626
47156CB00007B/2292